Katydid

Pine Ridge

Book Four

Ashley A. Quinn

TCA Publishing

ONE

A sharp whistle split the air, rising above the sound of hundreds of hooves pounding the muddy earth. A dog's bark joined the mix. The gray-blue and white heeler ran along the rear of the herd, nipping at the cattle when they tried to stray from the pack. Jasper Hendriks glanced over at his boss, Asa Mitchell, to see him gesturing to the left. Looking over, Jasper saw a steer running away from the herd. He spun his big gray gelding, Castle, toward the cow, cutting it off and shepherding it back into the fold. The animal bellowed its displeasure, sending glops of mud flying as he bucked while he ran back to his friends.

Jasper dodged a baseball-sized chunk and trotted back to his spot on the side of the herd. They were moving this group of yearlings to a different pasture that had a smaller pen attached, so the vet could do a herd check tomorrow. But this lot of steers wasn't having any of it today. All they wanted to do was run off and find the little shoots of grass emerging now that the snow had melted and the warmer spring temperatures had prompted plant growth.

Their newest hand, Tommy, opened the gate to the new

pen. Like a finely oiled machine, Jasper, Asa, and the handful of others with them kept the herd together as it funneled into the pen. Asa's dad, Silas, brought up the rear and latched the gate once the last steer went through.

"Whew." Jasper lifted his hat and wiped his sweaty forehead and face on his shoulder. "They were a rowdy bunch."

"For sure." Asa fanned himself with his hat. "I'm ready for a cold beer and some of Daisy's cookies."

"Sign me up." Both of those things sounded wonderful. So did getting out of this damp heat. It was mid-April, but it was steamy today. They'd had quite a bit of rain in the past week and the temperature today was in the lower seventies. It was muggy.

Jasper leaned back and reached into the small saddlebag attached to his saddle and withdrew a bottle of water. Gulping it down, his eyes wandered over the herd. They had a good crop of yearlings this year. All the steers were a nice size and looked healthy.

He turned toward the barn, ready to get off his horse and do something where there was a fan. It might not be beer and cookie time yet, but it was at least time to work on something else.

As they neared the barn, Jasper saw a sheriff's cruiser coming up the drive. "Hey." He called to Asa, then pointed to the car.

Asa's frown matched his. "What's a sheriff's deputy doing here?" He changed direction. "We better go see what this is about." He turned to Silas. "Dad."

Silas glanced over, and Asa tipped his head toward the driveway. Seeing the car, Silas nodded, and the three of them headed for the fence line.

Jasper dismounted and tied Castle's reins to the fence, then hopped over the rail. As his feet landed, he got a better look at the person behind the wheel and noticed it was the sheriff herself, Katy Lattimer.

"It's Katy," Silas said. "Maybe she's here to see Daisy? Or Sofie?"

She changed direction as she saw them walking toward her. The vehicle came to a halt ten yards away with a squeal of its brakes. The engine still running, the tall blonde sheriff emerged, a scowl on her pretty face.

"Don't any of you carry cellphones anymore?"

Jasper, Asa, and Silas shared a look.

"I had to call Daisy to find out where you were. She offered to call you on the radio, but by that point, I had called all of you and was almost here."

"We have them, but they don't always work, or we don't hear them. Why are you here?" Silas asked. "Is everything all right?"

"No. I need Jasper. We got a call about fifteen minutes ago to look for a pair of hikers who went up to Timber Point, but never made it back down."

Instantly on alert, Jasper straightened, his gaze sharpening. "When did they leave?" Jasper asked. He often worked search and rescue when needed in the area. If he wanted, he could run a search and rescue organization, but liked his job on the Stone Creek too much. He was content putting his tracking skills to use when they were needed.

"This morning. And before you ask, no, they didn't just decide to hike longer. One of them is a nurse at Pine Valley Medical. She was supposed to work a split shift with another nurse today, starting at four. She never showed up. That nurse called the woman's husband—who's on the hike with her—then the nurse's sister when she couldn't get ahold of the husband. The sister called us."

Jasper was moving toward her vehicle as she finished talking. He glanced back at Asa and Silas. "Can one of you take care of Castle for me?"

Asa nodded. "Yep. Stay safe."

He nodded and climbed into Katy's cruiser. "Can you swing past my house? I need to get my gear."

"Where is it? It might be faster for me to send a deputy to collect your things. I know for a fact Goodman can pick a lock." She glanced at him as she pulled away from the pasture.

"I live on the ranch." He pointed toward the main house and the cluster of smaller homes beyond it. "In those bungalows."

Bumping over the grass, she steered the SUV onto the lane that ran between the buildings. Jasper directed her to his white, single-story, two-bedroom house with its wraparound front porch. He was opening the car door as she put the vehicle in park.

"Give me five minutes." He glanced over his shoulder to see her nod. Dashing inside, he ran through the kitchen into the laundry room, then out the garage door to the loft storage, where he kept all his search and rescue gear. He grabbed the stepladder off the wall and set it up, scaling it so he could pull down a tub that contained his backpack, helmet, survival gear, a one-person tent, bedroll, and climbing harness. After snatching two bundles of rigging rope from the wall, he went back inside and raided his pantry for high-protein foods and water.

Piling everything on top of the tub, he went outside. Katy saw him coming and got out to open the liftgate. He set the tub in the cargo area and reached up to close the door. "I just need to change my clothes."

She nodded, and he took off for the house again. He knew time was of the essence. He wasn't holding out much hope they would find the couple before nightfall—it was already after five—but the less time they spent in the wilderness after dark, the better. In mid-April, nighttime temperatures hovered around freezing. Tonight would be a little warmer, but forty-five was still cold if you didn't have the right gear.

In his bedroom, he tugged off his boots and stripped out of his jeans and work shirt, leaving on the gray t-shirt underneath. He pulled on a pair of dark khaki cargo pants, then layered a gray thermal shirt over his t-shirt. Topping it off with a zip-up fleece, he shoved his feet in his hiking boots, tying them with swift movements, then grabbed his jacket, hat, and gloves and headed back to the car.

Two

Katy put the car in gear as Jasper buckled his seat belt. Casting a glance at him, she was surprised by the change in his appearance. He looked like a totally different man than the one who went into that house. It wasn't just his clothes, either. His demeanor had changed. Gone was the quick to smile, flirty man she'd gotten to know over the last few months. In his place was someone who reminded her more of her chief deputy, Ray Hughes. It was a rare day when she got him to smile at one of her jokes.

She blew out a breath. That was probably due more to the fact that she took what should have been Ray's job than his lack of a sense of humor. They'd made peace with the decision, but their relationship was strictly professional.

"You okay?"

She jumped. "Yeah." She kept her eyes on the road and blew out another breath.

"You sure? Because you don't look okay."

"I'm fine," she all but growled. "Just a little nervous about the search and rescue operation. I've worked plenty, but I've never been the point person."

"Do you have someone who can help you?"

"Yeah. My chief deputy. He's only run point once or twice in his career, but he helped Sheriff Lyons all the time." She brushed a stray hair away from her face. "Some days, I wonder what the county commissioners were thinking when they appointed me sheriff."

"You didn't have to accept the job if you didn't think you were ready."

"I know. But I was—am—ready. This is one of the few weak spots in my training. I might have been a dog handler in the Army, but I didn't do search and rescue. I was EOD."

"You were in explosive ordinance disposal?"

She glanced over at the note of incredulity in his voice, flattening her lips together as she took in the look of disbelief on his face. "That look right there is also why I took this job. Just because I'm young and pretty doesn't mean I'm not into things that go boom or that I can't be a good cop."

His expression cleared, and he winced. "Sorry. I knew you were military and a K-9 handler, but I guess I didn't think about what that meant. I didn't know you did explosives."

A dark shroud descended over her. "Yeah, well, I don't talk about it much." She preferred not to relive those memories.

"That bad, huh?"

"Yep."

"Forget I said anything."

"Good plan." She huffed and stared out the windshield, watching the road. Memories crowded in—ones she didn't want. She forced her mind onto a song, singing the lyrics in her head. She'd discovered a long time ago it helped refocus her mind and keep the bad stuff away.

The trailhead to Timber Point was only a fifteen-minute drive from the Stone Creek. Jasper pulled up a map on his phone while she drove, for which she was grateful. She didn't want to talk and risk getting onto a sensitive topic again. Her lack of sleep since she took the position as sheriff had brought back her nightmares, so it didn't take much for the memories to surface. She knew she should have dealt with them better years ago, but it had been easier to wall them off and pretend they weren't there.

When the trailhead sign came into view, Katy slowed down and turned right. She wound up the road through the trees until it opened up to the parking lot, which was rapidly filling with first-responders. She parked and they got out. Her eyes traveled over the assembly, landing on Chief Deputy Hughes. "This way." She motioned Jasper to follow and headed over to her deputy.

Hughes had a radio in his hand. Katy heard a male voice on the other end as she approached, but couldn't make out what he said.

"Any news?"

The deputy looked up as she came alongside him. "Sheriff. Jasper. No news yet." He waved the radio. "That was the fire department. They're bringing the SAR gear."

"I brought my stuff too." Jasper gestured to Katy's cruiser. "There any air support coming?"

"I called the state on the way up here. They're sending a chopper, but it'll be another half an hour before they're airborne. I'm not sure how much they'll be able to see, anyway. It's pretty dense up there."

It had been a hot minute since Katy hiked Timber Point, but she remembered the thick pine forest that gave it its name. Hughes was right; the chopper probably wouldn't be of much help. But they had to try.

"I'll gear up," Jasper said. "Once I get a team assembled, I'll head up the trail and see what I can pick up."

"Okay. John Danner and his K-9 unit are on their way, too, and so are the members of the county hasty teams."

"Good. I'm going to grab my gear." Jasper spun and jogged away.

Hughes held the radio out to Katy. "It's all yours, Sheriff."

Katy stared at it for a moment, then shook her head. "Actually, you keep it."

He frowned. "I'm sorry?"

"This is one area where you definitely have more experience than me. More skill. I'll serve this operation better if I go with Jasper." In addition to her EOD skills, she had extensive EMT training and had kept up her certifications. Katy was good under pressure and at managing people, but there were a lot of cogs in a search and rescue operation, and she wasn't as familiar with how they all worked as Hughes was. She knew she could figure it out, but she didn't want her learning curve to impact the rescue. Until she had more experience and training, Hughes was the best person to run point.

"You sure?" He pulled his arm back.

She nodded. "Yes. I'll take a radio and keep it tuned to what you're doing, so I can learn. I trust your judgment. What's the ETA on the fire department with the SAR gear?" She needed at least a helmet and climbing gear if she wanted to join Jasper on the mountain.

"Twenty minutes. They just left the station."

"Okay. Do we know the missing hikers' names?"

Hughes nodded. "Kayla and Derek Peterson."

"How about a map? Did you bring one with you?" She'd been out on patrol when the call came in, and the closest one to Jasper's location. When she couldn't reach him by phone, she'd detoured to get him, while Hughes drove up right away from town. She doubted he beat her to the scene by much.

He nodded. "It's in my cruiser. We can spread it out in the back while we wait for the command station equipment. It's with the fire department." He headed for his car.

Katy followed. He unrolled a topographical map over the

cargo area of his SUV, weighing it down with gear from the back.

"We're here." He pointed to a spot. "The trail winds up this way."

"That a map of the area?"

Katy glanced back to see Jasper peering over her shoulder. He had his climbing harness and helmet on now and was attaching a rope to his backpack as he spoke.

"Yeah." Hughes straightened. "We were just looking at the trail."

Jasper leaned in and traced an area with a finger. "I glanced at it on my phone in the car. The chopper will probably confirm it, but I'm betting there was a rock slide here. It's prone to slides, and with all the rain we've had on top of the snowmelt, I wouldn't be surprised at all to discover the trail covered. The question is whether they're stuck on the other side or whether they got caught in it."

Katy prayed they were just trapped on the other side, trying to find another way down. Or that they'd wandered off the trail and were lost. She didn't want to have to deal with more death. Not so soon after the two murders they had late last year.

THREE

Birds chirped around them, belying the seriousness of their hike as Jasper and Katy headed up the trail. So far, he'd seen plenty of evidence that the hikers ascended the trail, but nothing showing they made it down. A call just a few minutes ago on the radio confirmed his suspicions about a rock slide. The helicopter spotted it as it did its first pass over the area. It hadn't seen any sign of the missing hikers, though. Jasper wasn't all that surprised about that. The trees were dense. If they were trying to make their way around the slide, they would be deep in the forest, out of view from the air.

He glanced back, making sure Katy was keeping up. She was. Her blonde ponytail, peeking out from beneath her red helmet, glinted gold as the waning sunshine bounced off of it. She'd changed her gear for the hike, trading out her gun belt for a thigh holster. She'd also donned a climbing harness and a backpack full of supplies. Her long legs ate up the ground, staying right with him as he kept a punishing pace up the hill. They needed to reach the slide before dark so he could assess it. He hoped they could pick their way over it. If they had to go around, they'd lose precious time. Especially if they didn't go the same way as the hikers.

It took them just over thirty minutes to reach the slide. As it came into view, Jasper realized it was a big one. Much bigger than this area normally saw.

"Holy crap!" Katy stopped beside him.

"Yeah. It looks like half the hillside came down." Rubble obliterated the trail and piled a hundred feet high. He had no idea how deep it was. They couldn't see the hillside from their vantage point to tell.

"If they're under that, we'll never find them. Not without some serious heavy equipment and weeks of work."

If the forestry service could even get that kind of equipment up here. The trail wasn't built for excavation equipment. "Come on. I think I see a way up. Just watch your step." He walked forward and started picking his way over the loose rock to climb the pile. It was slow-going, but taking their time was better than rushing and ending up hurt.

Pebbles skittered down the hillside as they climbed. Jasper checked on Katy periodically, but the sheriff seemed confident as she picked her way up the rubble pile. Shadows grew as they ascended. He picked up the pace just a bit. The enormous pile seemed stable, so they could risk going faster.

Reaching the top, sunlight lit the rubble and the slope beyond. "Jesus." He stared over the expanse in front of them. A hundred-yard section of the mountain had collapsed.

"Wow." She glanced up at him. "Do we keep going?"

"Yeah. Let's see what we can find on the other side." He started forward. "Watch your step." Small rocks and dirt shifted beneath his feet as he made his way through the large boulders and trees to the other side. He paused at the edge and peered down.

"That's every bit as steep as the other side." Katy came up beside him to peer over the edge.

"Yeah." Jasper glanced back. "We need to find an anchor point. I'll climb up without a rope, but not down. Not on this." He spun away, eyeing the debris pile. A mostly intact tree about ten yards away, wedged between two giant chunks of rock, caught his attention. He scrabbled back over the rubble and unhooked his rope from his backpack.

"Do we have enough rope?" Katy took her rope off her pack and uncoiled it.

"Yes. But I think we'll need to tie on our second line before we reach the bottom." He wrapped his line, then hers, around the tree, securing them each with a hitch knot. "You ready?"

She nodded. Jasper liked the determination and confidence he saw in her eyes. He hadn't known what to expect with her, but she'd so far proven to be knowledgeable.

They walked back to the edge of the debris pile, then strapped themselves to their ropes. Jasper walked backward over the edge, placing each foot carefully. If he lost his footing, he'd drop several feet and probably slam into the wall of debris, even with his safety rope. He had no desire to show up at work tomorrow with giant bruises—or worse.

With careful steps, they walked down the wall. Twenty feet from the ground, they tied on their second lines and finished their descent. He unhooked himself from the rope and glanced around. Footprints marred the dirt on this side.

"Katy, look." He pointed to the trail. "They look like they belong to a man and a woman."

"That's good." She lifted her rescue whistle. "Time to see if they're close by." She blew into her whistle, giving it a few short, sharp blasts, then waited. They didn't know if the hikers had a whistle with them.

A sharp but faint retort echoed over the hillside. Jasper looked at Katy with a grin. "At least one of them is alive. Come on." He motioned down the hill. "It came from this way."

They followed the slide downhill. Jasper was amazed how

far it traveled. It flowed into a gully, then piled up, cutting off any escape route.

Katy blew her whistle again. Another return blast echoed, closer this time. They whirled, plunging into the growing darkness amongst the trees. Jasper broke out a flashlight. Every twenty feet, Katy blew her whistle until they could finally pinpoint the source of the sound.

"Oh, thank God!" A woman's voice sounded from the darkness.

Jasper's light bounced off a dark-haired woman's face. She sat on the ground next to a man, who leaned against a tree, his legs extended in front of him, one of them twisted at a gruesome angle.

Katy lifted her radio before Jasper could tell her to call for help.

"Hughes, it's Lattimer, over."

"Go ahead, Lattimer, over."

"We found them. Derek's got a badly broken leg. Can you get a chopper to drop us a basket? We scaled the debris and are on the other side. I brought smoke canisters, so I'll set one off when we hear the chopper inbound, over."

"Copy. I'll get the chopper to drop you the rescue basket. You need anything else? Over."

"No, over."

"Okay. Hughes out."

Jasper listened to her conversation with half an ear. Derek didn't look good. Pale and sweaty, he was clearly in shock. Kayla had done a good job trying to keep him warm with an emergency blanket, but his injury was taking its toll. "Hi. Kayla, right?"

The woman nodded.

"I'm Jasper. That's Sheriff Lattimer." He gestured with a quick tip of his head. "Can you tell me what happened?" He glanced at the woman.

She brushed her hair away from her face. "We were on our way back when we heard this terrible rumble. The ground shook and we just watched the side of the mountain fall away."

"You watched?" Katy crouched next to him and removed her pack.

Kayla nodded.

"How did this happen, then?" Jasper asked, pointing to her husband's leg.

"We were trying to find a way around it. He fell. I did what I could to keep him stable, but I think he's losing blood somewhere. I was about to leave him to climb higher so I could get a cell signal when I heard your whistle. How did you even know we were missing?"

"The nurse you were supposed to relieve called your sister when you didn't show up to work and didn't answer your phone. Your sister called us." Katy pulled a leg splint from her backpack along with a stethoscope and blood pressure cuff. "Mr. Peterson?"

The man trained pain-filled hazel eyes on her.

"I'm going to check your vitals, then stabilize your leg for transport. There's a chopper on the way." She wrapped a blood pressure cuff around Derek's arm and put the stethoscope in her ears.

Jasper watched her face as she listened. A frown formed between her eyes, and she looked up at him. A slight shake of her head was her only indication things were not well.

Kayla didn't miss it, though. "What? How bad is it?"

Katy's eyes met hers. "Eighty-eight over sixty." She pressed her fingers to Derek's wrist, looking at her watch, as Kayla gasped and blinked rapidly. "Pulse is one-twenty." She looked at Jasper, concern on her pretty face.

"You've got IV fluids in your kit, right?" Jasper pointed at her backpack.

"Yep." She was already opening the pack as he spoke.

"What can I do?" Kayla asked. "I want to help."

"You just keep him calm." She looked at Derek again. "I need to start an IV on you. We need to get your blood pressure up."

He nodded. Tears welled in his eyes, and he looked up at his wife. "I'm sorry, Kay. I should have listened to you."

She shushed him. "It's okay. You're going to be fine. The sheriff will get some fluids in you, then that helicopter will come whisk you off to the hospital."

Katy pulled on some gloves, then swabbed the crook of his elbow and took the cap off the needle. "Big pinch." She slid the needle into the vein.

Jasper picked up the clear bandage and opened the package. She took the dressing and spread it over the IV line. He tore some tape off a roll and handed it to her. She secured the dressing and the line, then tore open the bag of fluids and spiked it.

"Here." She passed the bag to Kayla. "Hold this. Jasper and I need to splint his leg."

Kayla took the bag. Katy dug into the EMT kit she'd shoved into her backpack before they took off up the trail. Jasper was impressed. She really knew her stuff. She made the right call, leaving Hughes in charge of the scene so she could come with him.

"I'm going to give you some pain medication. It'll make you feel woozy." She consulted the dosage chart and drew up the medicine, then added it to the port on the IV line. Almost immediately, Derek's body relaxed.

"You ready?" Jasper picked up the splint.

She nodded, putting the morphine away. "You lift, I'll slide."

He nodded as she took the splint. She spread it out on the ground next to Derek's leg. A touch of adrenaline pumped through Jasper's veins. Treating injuries always made him nervous. He didn't want to cause anyone pain. And moving Derek Peterson's leg was going to hurt. "Ready?"

"Yes. On three."

As gently as he could, he worked his hands under Derek's leg. They only needed a few inches. Just enough to slide the splint under him. "Okay. One... two... three." Jasper lifted. Derek groaned, but didn't pull away.

"I'm good. You can set it down."

Jasper lowered Derek's leg, then helped Katy form the splint around it. The man groaned again as the splint put pressure on his injured appendage.

"I'm going to radio back to base. See if I can get an ETA on that chopper." Katy got to her feet and walked several feet away.

He watched her go and considered her earlier fear that she wasn't fit to be sheriff. From what he'd seen so far today, she had all the qualifications necessary for a good leader. She'd put the people with the right qualifications in the places they needed to be—even though it removed her from the head of the operation—then demonstrated just how right she was. He couldn't imagine Ray Hughes performing the duties she just did, but he knew the man was a hell of a coordinator. Jasper was impressed with Katy's instincts.

Four

Breath puffing white in front of her face as she leaned against her cruiser, Katy brushed her hair back from her face. Her leg and back ached something fierce, and she knew she'd hobble around all day tomorrow like an old lady. As soon as she got home, she was going to take some maximum strength ibuprofen and sink into her jacuzzi tub.

"You okay?"

She jumped and turned her head to see Jasper walking toward her. She straightened, trying not to wince as her back twinged. "I'm fine. Just tired. Are you ready to go?" Derek and Kayla were at the hospital in Billings thanks to the state patrol's search and rescue helicopter, and all the searchers were back down the mountain and accounted for. She was ready to call it a day.

He nodded and cocked his head. "You want me to drive?"

Katy wiped any hint of pain from her face. "No." She turned and yanked on the door handle. "Let's go." Easing herself into the seat, she turned her face away in the guise of reaching for the door, so he wouldn't see her grimace. The pain receded to a dull roar as she settled into her seat. She blew out a breath, then started the car and put on her seat belt.

"Are you sure you're all right?"

"I'm fine." She said through clenched teeth. There was no way she would let on that her leg felt like it was on fire or that her back felt like someone gripped her spine in a vise. The old injuries flared whenever she overdid it, and today was a textbook definition of overdoing.

"If you say so."

She put the car in gear and drove out of the parking lot to take him home. The ride back to the Stone Creek was as quiet as the ride to the point. Katy was too tired to make small talk. All the energy she had left went into ignoring the pain coursing through her lower body and keeping her attention on the road.

Turning into the drive, she typed in the code Jasper rattled off, then drove through the gate and up the lane to his cute little bungalow. She liked his house. It was quaint and cozy, and she wondered if it was similar on the inside or if it was a bachelor pad.

In any case, she wouldn't find out tonight. "Thanks for your help today. I'm not sure Derek would have made it if you didn't find him as fast as you did."

He pulled on the door handle and the interior light came on, making his rich, dark hair shine in the artificial light, and looked back at her. Not for the first time, Katy was struck by how handsome he was.

"I'm glad I was around to help. You were good out there too. I knew you were a good cop—I saw you in action when you investigated Benny's murder and James's disappearance—but I had no idea you knew so much about emergency medicine or that you had such great climbing skills."

She blushed, uncomfortable with the praise. "Thanks."

He offered her a soft smile and swung a leg out of the car.

"Sure thing." He rose, then bent at the waist to look into the car. "Go home and take some pain meds. I hope your leg feels better."

Before she could respond, he shut the door, then went around back to get his gear box. Her mouth flattened as she watched him walk inside. She wasn't as adept at hiding her old injuries as she thought she was.

Or he could just be that perceptive. The man noticed bent blades of grass for crap's sake.

Scoffing at herself, she put the car in gear after he closed the door and waved. Turning around, she headed for the front gate and home.

The drive back to town was smooth, but long. Katy rolled the window down to help her stay awake, the blast of cold air refreshing. Turning onto her street, she slowed as her house came into view, then groaned as she saw the ancient gray Buick Regal parked at the curb. "Not tonight." Her grandma had a bad habit of just dropping by. Katy loved the woman to death, but tonight, she just wanted to sink into a tub full of bubbles, then go to bed.

She backed into the drive, parking her cruiser next to her grandma's car, then shut off the engine and got out. Limping, she walked up the sidewalk to the porch and let herself in the front door. The scent of stew and cookies hit her as she entered. Katy's stomach growled in appreciation. She hadn't eaten anything other than a protein bar on the hike since lunch.

"It's about time you came home. You're not the only person in the sheriff's department, you know." Heidi Beck waved an oven mitt at her from behind the counter in the kitchen, visible from the front door, then leaned down to remove a pan from the oven. Katy's house boasted an open floor plan, which she loved. It was light and airy and soothing after a long day at work. So was the scent of those cookies.

"Yeah, well, I'm the one in charge, so that means I have to make sure everyone else has what they need and has done what they're supposed to do before I can go home." She tossed her keys into the dish on the entryway table and sat on the bench to untie her boots. Her footwear probably had a lot to do with why her back and leg hurt so much tonight. Combat boots weren't the best thing for hiking over rough terrain. She was going to start leaving her hiking shoes in her car. She was still amazed she traversed that rock slide as well as she did in her clunky boots. "What are you doing here?"

"I heard about the missing hikers and knew you'd be late. And that you probably wouldn't bother to eat before you came home, so I brought you some stew and made some cookies."

Guilt hit Katy square in the gut. She should have known her grandma would do something like this. She did know. But fatigue wore her down and made her bitchy.

Sighing, she stood. "Thanks, Grandma. I'm going to put my gun away, then I'll be back." She strode down the hallway at the back of the great room to her bedroom on the right. Katy flipped on the light, illuminating the light blue walls and peach bedspread. The marbled gray rug covering part of the blonde hardwood floors was soft under her feet as she crossed to her nightstand. Opening the drawer, she laid her index finger on the scanner on her gun safe. The lid popped open, and she put the weapon inside, then closed it. After laying her gear belt on the chair by the window, she left the room. Her stomach was insistent she eat some of her grandmother's stew and cookies.

When she reached the kitchen, a bowl of stew, a chunk of French bread, and a beer waited on her at a seat at the island. She eased a hip onto the bar stool and tried not to wince as she sat.

"You tweak your back?"

Katy sighed and picked up her spoon. Getting one over on Grandma Heidi was never easy. The woman noticed everything. "And my leg. I had to scale a rock slide, and I wore the wrong shoes."

Heidi picked up a cookie. "Aren't you supposed to delegate that sort of thing now that you're sheriff?" She took a bite.

"Probably, but Ray's better suited to running a command center than me. I still need more training. Plus, we needed to get a medic in the field. The K-9 and hasty teams were still at least a half an hour away and we were losing daylight, so I went up the trail with Jasper Hendriks." She shook her head as she lifted a spoonful of stew and blew on it. "I knew the man was a good tracker, but damn. He's almost as good as a bloodhound." She slid the spoon between her lips, moaning as the flavors burst over her tongue. "This is so good. Thank you for bringing it."

Heidi beamed. "You're welcome, honey." Her smile slowly faded as she watched Katy eat. "You look terrible."

"Gee, thanks, Grandma." She rolled her eyes and ate another bite of stew.

"I mean it. You look like you haven't slept in weeks. Your nails are nonexistent, your hair needs trimmed, and the bags under your eyes could carry your entire wardrobe. I know you're new at being sheriff, but it can't honestly require you to work twenty-hour days, seven days a week."

It didn't, but Katy was doing her best to learn all there was to learn about being head of her department as well as do her normal cop duties. She needed more deputies, so she went out on patrol in addition to all her other sheriff stuff. "Until I get more manpower, it does. I still haven't found a deputy to replace me or the two that quit when the commissioners made me sheriff." She had a stack of applications on her desk, but finding time to review them was the problem. Katy scrubbed her face. Maybe she should just bring them home. They could be light reading while she relaxed in the tub.

Heidi scowled and picked up another cookie. "I can't believe you had deputies quit because the commissioners made you sheriff and not Ray. Though I suppose I should be happy. You don't have insubordinate employees to worry about now."

Oh, she still had plenty of those. They just needed their jobs more than the two who quit. But she was handling them. It helped that Ray was on her side. His willingness to accept her as the boss helped with the deputies who thought he'd been robbed of the job by a pretty face with boobs. Eventually, they'd come around, she suspected. But for now, she had to put up with them going to him first and the whispers behind her back that she wasn't good enough.

"It is what it is, Grandma. All that matters is that Ray and I have come to an understanding. He's the one I was truly worried about." Ray Hughes was a good man. And a good cop. She couldn't believe the commissioners chose her over him, either. But they wanted someone fresh, without personal ties to the old sheriff. Matthew Lyons had employed some—shady practices during his tenure as sheriff. There were times she hadn't agreed with his tactics or orders. She'd done her best to get around things she didn't agree with. She also knew if he hadn't passed away when he did, he'd have been looking at a recall election or even criminal charges. Ray had been quietly gathering evidence against him.

The commissioners didn't see it that way, though. They saw him as buddy-buddy with Lyons and viewed all the evidence he'd gathered as a ploy to make himself look good. If Katy was honest, she'd thought the same thing until she'd worked more closely with him and learned he was exactly what he said he was. She trusted him now.

"Well, I still think you need to find a way to not work so much. You need to sleep."

"I do sleep."

"More than a few hours a night."

Katy shoveled another bite of stew into her mouth and said nothing. Heidi frowned at her, but didn't say more, for which she was thankful. She didn't have the energy to argue.

"Do you want me to portion this out so you can take it to work this week?" Heidi gestured to the pot of stew on the stove.

"That would be great, actually. Thanks." It would be nice not to worry about making lunch for the next few days. And it would be a pleasant switch from the turkey sandwich she normally ate.

While Katy finished her dinner, Heidi found her stack of plastic containers and divided the stew among them. Snapping on the lids, she stacked them up and put them in the fridge.

"There. You're all set. I'll bag these cookies up, then be on my way so you can get to bed." She waggled a finger at Katy. "Do yourself a favor and don't get up before five tomorrow?"

Katy's face softened as she smiled at her. "I'll try." She was hoping for the same thing. But there was no guarantee her phone wouldn't ring before then.

Heidi studied her for a moment. "I'd tell you to turn your phone off, but I know you can't." She sighed, then walked around the island to press a kiss to the top of Katy's head. "I just worry about you."

"I know you do." Katy wrapped an arm around her grandma's waist and hugged her. "And I love you for it."

"Good." Heidi pressed another kiss to her head, then let go. "Because I'm going to keep doing it."

Katy chuckled. Heidi walked away to bag up the cookies she made. By the time Katy finished her food—cookies included—her kitchen was spotless once again.

"Thanks again for the stew and cookies." She took her bowl to the dishwasher and set it in the rack.

"Anytime, sweetie." Heidi headed for the front door, picking up her coat from the hooks over the bench. "Oh, I did a load of laundry for you too. You just need to put it in the dryer. I saw your hamper was overflowing when I cleaned your bathroom."

"Grandma! You didn't need to clean my house." Katy propped her hands on her hips and glared at the older woman.

Heidi snorted. "Like you have time to do it? And it only took me a few minutes. I just wiped things down. Swished the brush in the toilet."

"Still. I can clean my own bathroom."

"I know." She smiled as she shrugged into her coat. "Now you don't have to."

Katy sighed, her face relaxing as a rueful smile spread over it. "I love you, you know."

"I know that too." She picked up her purse. "I'll see you later. Lock up behind me." Heidi opened the door and let herself out with a quick grin and a wave of her fingers.

Chuckling again, Katy walked over and twisted the deadbolt, watching to make sure her grandma made it safely into her car. Katy flipped the porch light a few times. Heidi honked and drove away. The house felt quiet now without her grandma's bubbly personality in it.

Sighing, she pressed a fist to her aching back and limped toward the bathroom and that bath she promised herself.

FIVE

outh twisted as she bit the inside corner of her lip, Katy hovered the mouse over "Submit" on the registration form for a search and rescue conference in Salt Lake City next week. It was short notice, but the training would boost her confidence in dealing with situations like yesterday. She'd even pay for it out-of-pocket to offset the cost of overtime for the deputy needed to cover the shifts she'd miss. And she could take her laptop so she could keep up on reports.

She picked up her desk phone and punched in Ray's extension.

"Chief Hughes."

"Hey, can you come to my office for a minute? I want to run something by you."

"Sure. Be there in a second." He hung up.

Katy put down the receiver and scrolled the wheel on the mouse, staring at the screen. She glanced up as Ray appeared in her doorway, knocking on the jamb. She motioned him in. "Have a seat."

"What's up?" He sat down and rested an ankle over his knee, folding his hands over his abdomen.

"So, about yesterday. You know I'm not comfortable running SAR operations yet. Not the way I should be. There's a conference in Salt Lake next week I'd like to attend. If I go, though, that means you're on call as me while I'm gone, and we need to tap some deputies for overtime to cover the shifts I take on patrol. I'll still handle the business side of things from my laptop unless it's urgent. What do you think?"

He shrugged. "That's fine with me. And I know of a couple of deputies asking for overtime. We have the budget for the conference and the overtime?"

"No. I'll pay for the conference myself."

"If you can find the money for it, that's fine by me. I'll go talk to the deputies who wanted the hours and work on the schedule." He rose.

Katy smiled. "Thanks, Ray. I appreciate it."

"Sure." He waved a hand and left.

"Sweet." Katy clicked "Submit." That was one hole plugged in her skill set. Pushing away from her desk, she stood, wincing as her back twinged. The bath last night and pain meds helped, but she was still sore. She snagged her coat and put it on as she left her office. Her morning duties were done, so she was going out on patrol. On her way out of the building, she stopped by her admin's desk to let her know where she would be.

In her car, she logged in with dispatch, then pulled out of the lot. Out near the feed store, a dark blue truck turned from a side road onto the highway without stopping at the stop sign all the way. Katy slid in behind and turned on her lights, then called the plate in to dispatch and got out of her car.

The window rolled down as she approached and a man stuck his head through to look back. Katy raised an eyebrow and smiled as she saw who it was. "Jasper. Why are you running stop signs?"

That boyish, charming grin of his appeared. Attraction

flared low in her belly. She should give him a ticket just for that dangerous smile.

"Sorry. There was nothing coming."

She kept her face blank. "Maybe so, but you still have to stop. You got your license on you? And your registration and proof of insurance?"

His smile turned into a grimace. "Yeah. Hang on."

She bit back a grin, knowing full well she was only going to give him a warning. She'd let him stew a bit, though.

He poked his head back through the window and handed her the items she requested.

"Thanks. I'll be right back."

"Oh, take your time. I'm not eager to get that ticket."

She rolled her lips in and walked away, giggling once she was safely back in her cruiser. "Okay, Mr. Hendriks. Let's see what kind of driver you are." She ran his ID. Two speeding tickets—both paid—came up from the last ten years. He didn't have any other kind of record. Dispatch responded that his registration was valid. She grabbed her ticket book and walked back to his window.

"So how much of my money does the county get?" That boyish grin was back.

Katy smiled and shook her head. "None of it. You just get a warning." She handed him his paperwork, then opened the ticket book and wrote out the warning.

"Really? I thought you all had a budget crunch."

"We do, but that doesn't mean I'm going to give a ticket to a man who's only ever had two speeding tickets and saved two people yesterday. You mostly stopped. Next time, make sure the speedometer hits zero, yeah?" She ripped the paper from her book and held it out.

He took the pink paper. "Aw, you're just sweet on me, aren't you, Sheriff?"

Katy frowned. He couldn't possibly tell how that grin of

his made her feel. She'd kept her expression carefully controlled during their entire encounter. "Don't make me take that back and write you an actual ticket."

His deep chuckle reverberated through her chest. He held up his hands. "I'll behave."

"Good."

"I'm glad I ran into you, though. I was so focused on the rescue, it didn't really register what you were saying about wanting to improve your SAR coordinator skills. I mean, I heard you, but didn't plug it in to anything other than our conversation."

Katy frowned. "Huh? What are you talking about?"

He huffed a short laugh. "Yeah, I guess that didn't make a lot of sense. Anyway, short of it all is that if I hadn't been so focused on the SAR operation, I would have remembered to tell you there's a SAR conference in Salt Lake City next week that you might be interested in."

"Oh. Actually, I registered for it this morning."

"Really? That's great. I'm giving a talk on tracking."

Her eyebrows shot up. "You're speaking at the conference?" She was impressed. It was a regional conference, not just some local thing.

He nodded. "I have every year for the last five years."

She gave a rueful shake of her head as one side of her mouth rose. "You really are a bloodhound, aren't you?"

Jasper grinned. "Something like that. Hey, I'm driving down, are you?"

She nodded. It would be cheaper than flying and still only eat up a day.

"Want to go together to save on gas? It doesn't make sense for us to be going to the same place in separate vehicles."

Oh, that was tempting. Especially since the cost of the trip was coming out of her own pocket. But could she spend over ten hours confined in a vehicle with him? Twice? He made a good point, though. "I guess that would be all right. When did you want to leave?"

"As early as possible on Sunday. I'd like to relax and wind down some and then get a decent night's sleep before the conference kicks off Monday."

"Okay. We're still working on the schedule to get shifts to cover my absence on patrol, but I'll let you know."

"Sounds good."

She stepped back. "All right, well, I guess I'll see you in a few days, then."

He nodded. "Yep. Take care."

"You, too. And remember, speedometer to zero." She grinned.

He chuckled and gave her a quick two-finger salute. "Yes, ma'am."

Chuckling, she walked back to her cruiser as he drove away. As she sat down, she shook her head, hoping she wasn't making a mistake by agreeing to carpool to the conference. The man was dangerous to her equilibrium.

Six

A yawn stole over Jasper's face as he pulled into Katy's driveway. His morning hadn't gone as planned. After being awakened at two by a damn pack of coyotes, he had trouble falling back to sleep. Once he did, he hit snooze a few too many times, then had to rush to get ready. His first cup of coffee had been in the car instead of over breakfast, so his caffeine jolt hadn't kicked in yet.

Getting out of his truck, he crossed the yard and took the two steps to the porch and knocked on the front door. Through the frosted glass on either side of the dark wood door, he saw Katy's tall figure moving toward him. He heard the lock click, then the door opened.

His breath left him on a whoosh. Jasper was used to seeing Katy in her uniform. She was beautiful, no matter what she wore. But this morning, she was more than beautiful. She looked downright sexy. And she wasn't even trying. Curve-hugging jeans showed off her long, shapely legs, and a fuzzy-looking lavender sweater hinted at her curves beneath. Her long blonde hair was loose, feathering around her face in soft waves.

Swallowing the lump of attraction blocking his airway, he took a breath and stepped inside as she smiled a greeting.

"You look as tired as I feel." Katy shut the door and turned away, treating Jasper to a view of her butt. The uniform pants he normally saw her in didn't hold a candle to what those jeans did for it. He bit back a groan, not sure how he would survive being trapped in a car with her all day. He'd be lucky if he didn't need an ice pack on his groin by the time they made it to Salt Lake City.

She glanced back, a curious frown on her face. He averted his eyes from her butt just in time, catching the look she gave him. *She said something, didn't she?* Damn. He needed more coffee. And no more views of her perfect ass. Clearing his throat, he remembered what she said. "Nothing coffee can't fix. Are you ready to go?"

"Yes. I was just finishing my breakfast. Let me put my coffee cup and plate in the dishwasher, then we can go."

He followed her across the room to the kitchen, glancing around as he went. Wood beams crisscrossed the ceiling, adding dimension to the open room and echoing the deep color of the wood floors. Dusky emerald green cabinets popped against the white walls and quartz counters. Her living room boasted mahogany leather furniture and whitewashed wood tables clustered around a cream area rug. Accent pillows in burnt orange, and a deep blue added color to the space. So did the tiered wooden shelves overflowing with plants.

"I like your house. It's bright."

"Thanks. The openness is what attracted me to it. Other than some paint, the only change I really made was to replace the counters. They were a gray laminate."

Jasper ran a hand over the smooth quartz. "These are nice." He had black granite in his house, which suited him fine. He didn't care, really. His house was more just a place for him to hang his hat than anything else. It'd been a long time since he lived somewhere that felt like a home. Katy's house definitely felt like a home. She'd made it her own. It looked lived in. Comfortable.

Ceramic clanked as she added her breakfast plate to her dishwasher. He glanced away, unable to take another view of her butt, as she bent over to put a detergent tab in the door, then shut it. His eyes landed on her refrigerator. It was covered in pictures.

"Who are all these people?" He stepped closer to get a better look.

"Friends and family."

He saw one of her in a cap and gown, standing with a man in uniform who looked to be a couple of years older than her. "Who's this?"

She walked over to look at the picture he pointed at. "My brother, Marcus." She pointed to a different one. "That's my grandma, and my mom and dad."

"Wait. Heidi Beck is your grandma?" He knew the older woman. She used to teach English at the local high school. He never had her, because he grew up in Billings, but his sister did. He heard a lot about Mrs. Beck and the crazy ways she got students interested in the materials she taught. There were a lot of costumes involved.

Katy smiled, heaving a sigh. "Yes, she is. I see her reputation precedes her. Did you have her in high school?"

"No. I went to school in Billings. My sister had her, though. Her junior year, I think."

"Lucky girl. Grandma's class was the most sought after in the school." She stepped away from the fridge and picked up a travel mug before heading for the entryway. "I didn't get to be in her class because she was my grandmother, but I got to help her with costumes and skits. That was just as fun."

"I bet. Megan loved her class." They stopped in front of her bags. "This all you have?" He lifted her suitcase.

She nodded. "Just that and this." She pointed to a large tote, then set her coffee down and took her coat off the hook to put it on.

Jasper headed for the door. She picked up the tote, her purse, and her coffee, then followed, locking the door behind them.

He took her tote from her and put it and her suitcase in the backseat with his bag while she got into the passenger seat. Once they were both ensconced in the front of the cab, he started the engine and backed out of her driveway.

It didn't take long for her scent to permeate the truck. It was something soft and uniquely feminine. Jasper gritted his teeth. It shouldn't have overpowered the smell of fresh coffee, but it did. Maybe he was just extra sensitive to it, thanks to his attraction to her.

He shifted in his seat. *Definitely going to need that ice later.*

Seven

A hard jolt brought Katy awake. Her eyes popped open, and she looked around, disoriented.

"Sorry. I didn't see the pothole until it was too late." Jasper glanced at her, his expression apologetic.

She rubbed her eyes and looked out the window. They were no longer on the interstate. "Where are we?"

"Idaho Falls. We need gas. And I'm starving."

Katy looked at the clock on the dash. "Oh, wow. I slept a while. Why didn't you stop earlier if you're so hungry?"

He shrugged and turned off into a gas station that boasted a fast-food restaurant. "You looked tired, so I let you sleep."

"Well, thanks." She did feel more rested now. As she should after a two-hour nap.

Jasper pulled up to a pump and cut the engine.

"I'll go order our food while you pump gas, if that's all right? We can keep our receipts and total everything up when we get home, then figure out who owes who what."

He nodded and pulled on the door handle. "Works for me. Double bacon cheeseburger with the works, fries, and a soft drink, please."

"Okay. What kind of soda?"

"Diet Pepsi or Diet Coke. Whichever they have."

She gave him a thumbs up and climbed out, hurrying across the parking lot to get out of the wind. She was glad he was the one pumping gas and not her. It was chilly here. She wished she'd put her jacket on before she got out of the truck.

The bell dinged on the door as she stepped inside. Shaking off the chill, she walked toward the restaurant, groaning as she saw the line. She had to pee and did not want to stand there for the next fifteen minutes waiting to order with a full bladder.

Katy spun around and found the restrooms. She'd pee first, then go stand in line.

Once she finished her business, she washed her hands. As she dried them, the sound of raised male voices drew her attention. Frowning, she tossed her paper towel in the trashcan and moved toward the door. Their tone was angry. Automatically, her hand went to her hip, and she cursed as she remembered she left her gun in the truck beside Jasper's concealed carry in the console, but neither of them helped her all the way out in the parking lot.

She nudged the door open. The arguing grew louder. From her vantage point, she could make out several patrons staring toward the drink case. A little girl clutched her mother's leg, peeking out from behind it at the altercation taking place.

A young man in his twenties, red-faced, screeched at a trucker. A vein pulsed in the older man's temple as he stared the younger man down.

Katy approached, cautious. Without her weapon, things could get out of control quickly if one of them drew a knife or a gun. She needed to rely on her training to defuse the situation.

The bell dinged over the door. She saw Jasper enter and

pause as he heard the commotion. The pair arguing paid him no heed. Before she could tell him to stay put, he walked over to her.

"What's going on?"

"Not sure. I heard them arguing while I was in the restroom. I was about to attempt to defuse things."

"Okay. If things get physical, I'll take the trucker. You get the kid."

She nodded and stepped forward. "Gentlemen, let's take things down a notch, okay? There are children here, and you're scaring them." She motioned to the woman with the little girl.

The younger man turned his fiery gaze on her, mouth twisted in an ugly scowl. "Stay out of this, bitch."

"Can't do that, sorry."

"Ma'am, he's right. This doesn't concern you." The older man held out a hand, waving her off.

"It does when you're arguing in the middle of a gas station. So," she glanced at the younger man, "how about you tell me what's got you so worked up?"

The man rolled his eyes. "Pops here took the last can of the energy drink I wanted."

Katy did a double-take. *Was he for real?* "You're screaming at him in public because he took the last energy drink?"

He bounced on his toes and ran a hand under his nose as his eyes went from her back to the trucker. "Yeah. Dude told me 'you snooze, you lose, kid.'" He scoffed. "I ain't gonna take that crap from some old man. And I ain't no kid." He took a step toward the trucker.

"Boy—" The trucker stepped forward, fist raised.

Katy shot a hand out and shook her head. The older man paused.

"What's your name?" She tried to refocus the younger man's attention. His jitters told her he was probably high on something. She needed to distract him and get the trucker out of here to de-escalate things.

"None of your business, bitch. I told you to beat it."

"Right. I'm still not going anywhere. So, what's your name?"

He glared at her and shifted his weight, picking at his face again.

"Come on, you gotta give me something to work with. I can't call you Blondie. That's what they call me."

A corner of his mouth kicked up, and a predatory gleam entered his eyes. "I can think of a few other things to call you, babe."

A low growl came from behind her. She felt Jasper shift closer and prayed he wouldn't try something. She still didn't know if either of them had a weapon.

"I'm sure. And I've probably heard them. I'd still rather people used my name. It's Katy. What's yours?"

His eyes shifted from her to glance around the gas station, then back. "Bryce."

"It's nice to meet you, Bryce. How about we find you some other energy drink and get you and this other gentleman on your way?"

"I want that one!" He pointed to the can in the trucker's hand.

"Well, tough shit, kid. I ain't giving it to you." The trucker crossed his arms and glared.

The younger man lunged. Katy dove forward, snagging him around the waist, taking him to the ground. He grappled with her, striking out with one long arm. His fist glanced off her jaw, and she knew she'd have a bruise tomorrow. She grabbed his wrist and pushed it down, straddling his hips. Torquing his arm, she rolled him onto his stomach just as she heard sirens outside. It was all over in just a few seconds.

"Let me go, bitch! This is assault! I wanna press charges!"

She brought his other hand up, holding them both in one of hers, and leaned down, pressing her forearm into his shoulder blades to hold him to the ground. "Good luck with that."

Two police officers entered the store. She heard other customers direct them to her, and glanced back as they approached, tossing her head to get her hair out of her eyes. Both cops paused and stared at her for a moment.

"I'm Sheriff Katy Lattimer. Campbell County, Montana. My badge is in my purse." She tipped her head toward the bag still slung across her shoulders.

"You're a cop? No fucking way!" The man beneath her squirmed.

She shifted and pressed her knee into his back. "Hold still." She glanced at the two officers watching. "One of you want to cuff this kid?"

The men jumped into action. One of them kneeled beside her to handcuff the young man, while the other helped her hang onto his arms. Once the cuffs were on, she stood up, lifting the man off the ground. She handed him off to one of the officers, who escorted him out of the building.

The other one watched his partner for a moment, then turned to her. "Can you tell me what happened?"

She relayed what she'd heard from the restroom and what happened after she emerged. The man took notes, nodding as she talked.

Once he had the full story, he looked up, glancing around. "Where's the trucker?"

Katy scanned the store and saw him near the cash register. "Over there." She dug her business card out of her purse and handed it to him. "If you need anything further, call my office. I'll be out of town for the next few days, but they'll be able to reach me."

He nodded, taking it from her as he looked away from the trucker.

"Yes, ma'am. I just need you to write out a statement for me now and that should be it."

Katy nodded, then looked at Jasper, who'd been silent since she took the man to the ground. "Do you want to give a statement?"

"Don't know what I'd say. I didn't do anything. Just watched you be your badass self."

She blushed and smiled. "It would just corroborate my version of events."

He shrugged. "Sure."

"Let me go get the reports from the cruiser. I'll be right back." The officer put his notebook in his pocket and walked away, stopping to speak to the trucker before leaving the store.

Katy pressed her fist into her back.

"You okay?"

"Yeah. Is there a hot tub at the hotel we're staying at?"

"Maybe. I'm not sure."

She hoped there was. It'd be roomier than the bathtub. She'd be able to float and the jets would help relax her muscles.

Jasper's stomach growled, and she chuckled.

"What? I told you I was hungry. That hasn't changed." He hooked his thumbs in his pockets, a corner of his mouth lifting.

"Nice to know adrenaline doesn't curb your appetite."

"No. If anything, I'm hungrier."

The officer walked back in, carrying a metal storage clipboard. As he came closer, he lifted the lid and withdrew two forms. "Here you go. I only have one pen, though."

Katy took a paper and the pen. "We'll go ask the clerk for another. Thanks." They wandered away to get another pen, then took seats in the small restaurant to write down what happened. Once they finished, they signed the forms and took them back to the officer, who was finishing up with the trucker.

He held out a hand. "Thank you for intervening. My partner found a knife in the kid's pocket. Things could have turned out much differently."

Jasper stiffened beside her. She cast him a curious look, then took the officer's hand. "You're welcome. I'm glad I was here to help."

He thanked her again, then turned back to the trucker. Katy blew out a breath and turned, heading for the restaurant again so they could finally get some lunch. Jasper wasn't the only one who was hungry.

The line had dissipated with the commotion, so they were able to order right away. She added an ice cream sundae to her order, figuring she deserved it after having to work when she wasn't working. They took their drink cups and filled them while they waited, then leaned against the wall. She glanced up at Jasper and noted the hard set to his features.

"What's wrong?"

"Nothing."

His short reply told her he was lying. "Uh-huh. You forget I deal with criminals for a living and can spot a lie a mile away. Try again."

His jaw worked. "Don't worry about it. I'll be fine."

Katy opened her mouth to reply, but the woman at the counter called her name. She snapped her mouth shut, pressing it into a firm line. Giving him a frown, she went to get her food.

Eight

Jasper watched Katy walk away as he vibrated with the urge to punch something. Or someone. That kid who brought a knife into a convenience store and picked a fight with a trucker twice his size would work.

The woman at the counter called his name. He walked up to get his food, then followed Katy to a booth and slid in across from her, keeping his eyes down. He didn't want her to see the anger simmering in his gaze. It wasn't directed at her.

"Okay. Why won't you look at me? Or talk to me? What did I say?"

He glanced up, but looked out at the parking lot. "You didn't say anything. This is my problem, not yours." And it was. He was angry that she could have been hurt. Even though he knew full well she could take care of herself, the thought that that punk could have pulled his knife at any time and stabbed her churned in his belly like bad sushi.

"What? What are you talking about?"

He took another bite of his sandwich, debating how to answer. He really didn't want to get into why that made him so angry. Finally, he looked at her. "It's nothing. I'll be fine. Can we talk about something else?"

She frowned at him, but nodded after a moment. "Sure. Such as?"

He shrugged and ate some fries.

Katy huffed and stuffed a fry in her mouth. "Tell me about your sister. She's younger than you?"

Jasper nodded, relieved she'd changed the subject. "Yeah. Quite a bit, actually. My mom had a one-night stand in college with some douche bag fraternity kid, and I was the result. He didn't want anything to do with me. She didn't marry until I was ten. I was twelve when Megan was born."

"Oh, wow. I bet that was strange for you."

"Kind of. But she's a great kid."

She took a sip of her drink. "So, when did you all move to Pine Ridge?"

"Mom and Megan moved to town about a year after I started college. My stepdad died in a car accident, and Mom took a job here at the resort." He paused and glanced out the window again as emotion sucker-punched him. Drawing in a breath, he pushed past the lump in his throat. "I moved here two years later when she passed away from breast cancer. I didn't want to take Megan away from her friends."

Katy's eyes went wide. "Wait. You raised your little sister?"

He gave a quick nod. "From the time she was nine, yes."

"Wow. Jasper—that's incredible. I can't imagine being a parent to a nine-year-old at the age of, what, twenty-one?"

"Yeah." He rolled his lips in, nodding. "My mom's parents disowned her when she got pregnant with me. And Kevin's parents—Megan's dad—they were older and couldn't really take care of her. And they lived in Billings. Megan had a life in Pine Ridge. Friends. After all she'd lost, I didn't want her to lose that too. The only other option was foster care. So, I quit school and moved into Mom's house. Silas gave me a job." He shrugged. "We had our ups and downs as we adjusted, but we made the best of it, and I don't regret any of it. She was worth it." That was no lie. Jasper loved his sister with a fierceness he hadn't known about until they were all each other had. He'd do anything for her.

Katy cleared her throat. "That's really great. So, what were you studying in school?"

"Mechanical engineering. Though I didn't expect to really use my degree. I had a full-ride on a baseball scholarship and a good chance to turn pro." He shrugged. "I guess I was wrong. I use a lot of the knowledge I gained still today."

"Well, I'm happy things worked out for you and her. Even if it isn't quite what you planned."

"Me too." He took another bite of his burger, his heart heavy with thoughts of his mom. But there were happy thoughts too. From when she was alive, and later, when it was just him and Megan. He was proud of how far they'd come.

Finished with their food, they made their way back out to the truck.

"Can I drive?" Katy paused in front of the hood and looked up at him.

"Sure." He unlocked the car and climbed into the passenger seat. A nap sounded nice. Between the riot of emotions that flowed through him in the last hour and the food, he was in need of a recharge.

She got in next to him. After adjusting the seat and mirrors, they were back on the road.

Jasper grabbed his sunglasses and popped them on, then leaned his head back. "Wake me when you need me to take over." He registered the quick nod of her head, then closed his eyes. The radio came on to some country station, and he let the music lull him into sleep.

NINE

The hotel room door snicked closed as Katy stepped into the hallway. Pain radiated up her leg with every step she took toward the elevator. When they checked in, she'd been pleased to discover the hotel had a hot tub. She planned to take full advantage of it right now.

With a ding, the elevator doors swished open and she stepped inside, pushing the button for the ground floor. It was a short ride down from the fifth. She stepped off, doing her best to keep her gait as normal as possible. Limping just made her back hurt more and didn't take away all the pain in her leg.

She turned down a short hallway to the pool area and let herself inside. Children's shrieks bounced off the walls and the strong scent of chlorine assailed her. Sticking to the perimeter, she headed for the hot tub along the far wall. A man sat in it. She almost turned around, not wanting to deal with some stranger ogling her in her swimsuit, but the pain shooting through her leg and the ache in her back kept her moving forward. She'd just deal with it if he was an asshole.

Rounding the hot tub, she set the towel she carried on a chair, then stepped out of her sweats and t-shirt, revealing her black one-piece suit. She steeled herself against any interested looks or comments and turned. The man lounging against the far side smiled at her, his eyes raking her body. Katy stepped into the steamy water and quickly sank up to her neck, hiding herself from his view. She tipped her head back against the padded headrest, closing her eyes, and sighed. The pain in her back and leg receded.

"Long day?"

Katy grunted an affirmative but kept her eyes closed.

"A hot tub sure is a great way to relax. Follow it up with a drink from the hotel bar—maybe some polite conversation." He sighed. "You can't beat that."

Her teeth clenched at the flirty note to his voice, and she opened her eyes to pierce him with an icy glare. "Sir, I don't want to talk. I just want to let the water work its magic."

"Ah." He smiled. "So she does speak."

Katy resisted the urge to growl. Closing her eyes, she let her head fall back again, determined to ignore him.

"You here by yourself?"

She snorted. Like she'd answer that question, even if she was interested in him. That was the quickest way to get herself a stalker.

"She's not, no."

Her eyes snapped open. An upside-down image of Jasper filled her vision. He stood behind her, a steely edge to his gray eyes as he stared at the man. She lifted her head to turn around. "What are you doing down here?"

"Figured I'd join you. It was a long ride." He slid his feet out of his running shoes and peeled his gray t-shirt off, tossing it onto the chair with her clothes.

Katy's mouth went dry as all the moisture rushed south. Hot damn! She knew he was muscular. It was hard not to notice beneath his clothes. But holy hell! Without his shirt he was magnificent. He put all the underwear models to shame.

Every dip, every ridge and swell of muscle stood out in stark relief beneath a smattering of dark hair on his chest. A happy trail split his perfect abs to disappear beneath the waistband of his navy-blue swim trunks, which stopped midway down his thick, muscled thighs.

He stepped into the water and sat down beside her, his shoulder touching hers. "Oh, that feels nice." He stretched out his long legs and let his hands float, then looked at her. "Are you feeling better?"

She swallowed, beating back the flutters in her belly trying to climb her throat and block her airway. The man was lethal. "Um, yeah. The pain's gone. It'll come back once I get out, but it shouldn't be as bad."

"Good." He gave a short nod, then laid his head back.

Katy mimicked his pose, and her eyes landed on the man across from them. He frowned now, looking perturbed. She knew she shouldn't feel so glad that Jasper made him feel inadequate, but she didn't appreciate being hit on. Especially after she made it clear she wasn't interested.

Jasper leaned closer. Tingles raced along the back of her neck as his warm breath fanned the wispy hairs on the side of her face.

"I don't really have anything to say, but I want to make the dude uncomfortable, so he'll leave," he whispered in her ear.

It took a moment for his words to register through the fog of lust that had descended on her. When they did, she laughed.

His deep chuckle mingled with hers. "I vote that after this, we order a pizza and find some terrible movie before we crash. Or a sitcom. I could go for funny."

Smiling now, and more relaxed, she turned her head, intending to ask him how he knew she was down here, but got lost in his eyes. Katy's smile slowly died. Caught in his gaze, heat built, threatening to set her ablaze.

Water splashed as the man across from them stood up. "Geez, get a room."

Jasper didn't look away. "We have one."

More water splashed as the man walked out of the hot tub.

Katy inched away, trying to put a rein on her wild attraction to the man beside her. Good Lord. She thought she'd go up in flames there for a moment. Closing her eyes, she tried to relax again.

"So, how'd you injure yourself?"

So much for relaxing. Katy blew out a breath. "It's an old injury. From my military days."

"The ones you don't want to talk about?"

"Those are the ones, yes." She really didn't. Those were memories better left buried.

"You sure? Talking about trauma's supposed to be good for you."

Her eyes snapped open again as anger surged. "Do you want to know to help me or for your own curiosity?"

Steady eyes met hers. "Both."

She huffed. At least he was honest. "There was an IED. It blew up. My dog died and so did my teammates. Happy?"

"No. Your pain doesn't make me happy, Katy. I just wanted to make you feel better."

"Yeah, well, talking about it makes me feel worse."

"Because you haven't dealt with the memories."

"How would you know?"

"Because I've been in your shoes. I lost my mom when I was twenty-one and took on my nine-year-old sister. Trust me. I know." He was silent a moment, making figure eights in the water with his hands. "I was so busy those first couple of years trying to learn how to be a parent, I didn't give myself time to grieve."

He paused his movements and looked at her. "Then Megan hit puberty. She threw some barbs at me when she was hormonal that hit the quick." He rubbed a fist over his heart. "Told me Mom wouldn't have been so hard on me. That she was a better parent than me. Duh. I was barely old enough to have an infant, let alone a tween. After one particularly loud fight, she stormed out. I let her go. We both needed to cool off, and I knew she'd probably just head to her friend Mandi's house. Once my anger cleared, all those emotions I bottled up burst free, and I sobbed like a baby."

Katy balled her fists to keep from touching him. She didn't want to disturb the flow of words.

"When she finally came home, I just hugged her tight and told her I was sorry. That I was trying the best I could." He waved his hands through the water again, some of the tension leaving his shoulders. "She apologized too. Said she talked to her friend about how much she missed Mom and not having an adult female to talk to. We came to an understanding after that. That we both needed to cut each other some slack. That we were both still grieving."

He fell silent. Katy processed what he said. And what he didn't. She still couldn't fathom doing what he did. The courage it took to alter his entire life at such a young age to take on the responsibility of a child. Not an infant he could grow with, but an older child.

She also couldn't help but see that by sharing his story, he was encouraging her to open up about herself. But if she tore off those bandages, she wasn't sure she could stop the bleeding.

"Thank you for sharing that." Her voice was soft, barely audible over the bubbling water. "I know you think I need to let it all out, but I—I just can't." Emotion clogged her throat, cutting off her words.

"Hey." He took her hand under the water. "It's okay. One day, when you're ready, you'll talk about it. Whether that's to me or someone else, I don't know. And it doesn't really matter. You'll share it with whomever you think you should when you think the time is right."

Katy nodded, looking down at their clasped hands beneath the water. She didn't trust her voice to speak.

He nudged her with his shoulder, still holding her hand. "So what do you want on your pizza?"

A startled laugh burst from her chest. "Do you ever think of anything besides your stomach?"

"Oh, baby, if you only knew."

The quick flash of heat in his eyes told her all she needed to know. A blush stained her cheeks, and she glanced away with a nervous chuckle. "Never mind. I don't want to know. And pepperoni is fine." She tugged her hand from his in the guise of shifting her position. She needed some distance if she wanted to hang on to her sanity. His overt sexiness—not to mention his kind heart—were threatening to do her in.

"Playing it safe, huh? Do you like spicy food?"

"Depends on the food. I'm not a big fan of spicy Mexican. I think the flavors are great without the heat. But Indian or Moroccan? The heat is ingrained in some of those dishes, and they are magnificent."

"Moroccan? I've never had that. I've had Indian, though."

"It's not that dissimilar. Not as spicy. More beef. Couscous instead of rice. They both use a lot of the same spices, though, just in different proportions and combinations."

"I'll have to give it a shot if I ever come across a Moroccan restaurant."

"There are probably some here. We should go to one."

"I'm game." He sank deeper into the water and groaned. "Tomorrow, I'm game. I'm going to be too relaxed to walk before long. I need to add one of these to my house."

Katy chuckled. "Me too. I've actually been saving up for one. My big bathtub works for now, but sometimes, I just want to float."

"Well, let's take full advantage of this one while we're here."

"Oh, I plan to."

They soaked another fifteen minutes, then Jasper's growling stomach got to be too much for either of them to take. Katy could hear it over the water and the sound of the few kids playing in the pool. "Come on." She stood, water sluicing down her long body. "Let's go feed that beast making so much noise."

Chuckling, he rose beside her. She glanced away, but not before she got an eyeful of his chiseled body, dripping wet, and his swim trunks clinging to his hips. Suddenly, she was hungry for much more than food. Cheeks flushing, she hurried from the water and the temptation that was Jasper Hendriks.

TEN

oly hell. Jasper tried not to stare as Katy stepped out of the hot tub. Water cascaded off of her lithe, athletic body. The black one-piece suit she wore molded to her butt, showing off the supple muscles of her hips and thighs. His eyes traveled lower, down her mile-long legs, pausing on the scars marring her left calf and ankle.

It was like a cold bucket of water over his head, dousing the fire burning in his blood and reminding him why she was in the hot tub to begin with. And of the heavy conversation they had just a few minutes ago.

He followed her out, drying off with the towel he brought. Katy wrapped her towel around herself and picked up her clothes. Jasper put his shirt on and stuffed his feet in his shoes.

"Ready?"

She nodded.

They left the pool area and headed for the elevators. He pushed the button for the fifth floor and watched the gauge tick off the floors as they rose. The ding announced their arrival, and they stepped off. The clerk put them on the same floor across from one another. Jasper paused in front of his door, key card in his hand. "I'll order us a pizza. You want to eat in your room or mine?"

"Yours." She made a face. "I have noisy neighbors."

His eyebrows went up, but he didn't ask any questions. "Okay. Come over in about ten minutes? I'm going to order food and hop in the shower."

She nodded and slid her card into the reader, disappearing behind her door. Jasper entered his room, glad for the reprieve, even if it was short. He needed a few minutes to get himself under control. Between the emotion dump he'd just done and watching her parade around in that swimsuit with her mile-long legs on display, he was hanging on by a thread.

Tossing his key card, wallet, and phone onto the bureau, he picked up the room phone and called the front desk to get the number for a local pizza place that delivered. The man who answered gave him the number for a restaurant just around the corner. Jasper called it to place an order.

Once the food was on its way, he grabbed some clean clothes and went into the bathroom. He stripped out of his t-shirt and wet swimsuit and hung the trunks over the bathtub, then turned on the shower and stepped into the spray. It hit him like a thousand icy needles, but he didn't care. The chilly water helped calm what was left of the fire in his blood.

Jasper soaped his body, washing off the chlorine, then shut the water off and toweled down before dressing in a pair of athletic shorts and a t-shirt. He didn't plan on going anywhere else tonight and wanted to be comfortable after the long day of traveling.

His phone dinged as he emerged from the bathroom. He picked it up to see a text from his sister. She was responding to his earlier message that they made it to Salt Lake in one piece. As he sent her a smiley face emoji, a knock sounded on his door.

Pocketing his phone, he answered it. Katy waltzed past

him, a bag of candy in her hands. The scent of her peach shampoo hit him as she walked past, reigniting the fire he'd managed to bank. The sight of her bare legs didn't help, either. Like him, she wore shorts and a t-shirt, but her gray shorts stopped just above mid-thigh whereas his hit just above his knees. The light blue t-shirt she had on wasn't much better. It hugged her full breasts and made his mind go back to the sight of her in her modest, but still revealing swimsuit.

Christ. Get it together, man. He shook his head to clear it as he closed the door. "Pizza's on its way," he told her. "They'll call from downstairs when they get here."

"Sounds good. I'm hungry. I brought a snack to tide me over." She rattled the bag of Skittles. "Want some?" She sat on his bed and opened it.

"Did you bring that with you from home?" He sat next to her and held out a hand. It wasn't one of the regular ones in the vending machines. It was the kind with the zipper seal.

A sheepish grin covered her face. "Would you think less of me if I said yes? I love Skittles. I keep bags everywhere. I even carry a bag in my purse. I packed this one special, though." She tipped some into his palm.

Jasper tossed a red one in his mouth. "I haven't had these in forever."

"No?"

He shook his head. "I don't eat a lot of candy anymore. Daisy makes cookies, so usually when I want something sweet, that's what I have."

She snickered. "I'd just add them to my Skittles addiction."

He grinned and popped a couple more pieces of candy into his mouth.

"We need drinks. I don't suppose you ordered any soda or water, did you?"

"No. We can get it from the vending machine, or from the little shop in the lobby."

Her head bobbed, and she ate another Skittle, then abruptly closed the bag and stood. "Let's go see what they've got."

"Now?" He stared up at her, confused by the sudden shift.

She shrugged. "Might as well. Maybe the pizza will show up while we're down there."

Jasper decided to just go with the flow. For whatever reason, she obviously couldn't sit still quite yet. "Let me put my shoes on." He dug a pair of socks out of his suitcase, then put on his running shoes. "Okay. Let's go." Swiping his wallet, phone, and key card off the dresser, he followed her out the door.

They rode down to the lobby and strolled through the few guests downstairs to get to the small store near the restaurant, where they each bought a water. While they waited, they stopped by the front windows and looked out over the parking lot and the highway beyond. Even with the urban sprawl, it was pretty here. It looked like home, but didn't.

Jasper saw a few people he knew while they wandered and said hello, introducing Katy. The instructor for the course she planned to take on crisis center management walked past, and Jasper nudged her.

"That's Gary McCarthy. He's teaching your crisis management seminar."

"Oh?" She turned to watch the man walk across the lobby. "Is he a decent teacher?"

Jasper nodded. "Yeah. You'll learn a lot from him. He knows his stuff and can convey it to others well."

He was happy to see the frown between her eyebrows smooth out some. He knew she had high hopes for this conference.

The pizza delivery driver walked through the front doors,

garnering their attention. Jasper flagged him down and paid him, then they went back upstairs. His stomach growled the whole way back, making Katy chuckle.

"I hope you never have to hide from something or someone when you're hungry. You will not survive."

He chuckled and unlocked the door. "That's no lie." Entering the room, he set the box down on the long counter by the coffeemaker. The pizza parlor sent paper plates and napkins, and he handed a plate to Katy. She opened the box and put two slices on it, then grabbed a napkin. Jasper loaded his plate, then turned to find a place to sit. Katy had parked herself in the middle of the bed, legs crossed. She wrapped her lips around a slice and moaned.

"Oh, that's delicious."

Jasper clenched his teeth and marched over to the chair in the corner. She had zero idea how sexy she was.

"So, what do you want to watch?" She picked up the remote, holding her pizza in her other hand, and turned on the TV.

He shrugged. "Something funny."

Her head bobbed once, and she pulled up the guide. "How about *Friends*?"

"Sure." He took a bite of his food, holding back a moan of his own. She was right; it was very good.

"Jasper?"

"Hmm?"

"How are you going to watch TV from over there?"

He glanced at the television. From where he sat, he could barely make out the screen. He scanned the room and frowned. Even if he moved the chair, he couldn't move it far enough to get a good angle. There just wasn't space. The only decent vantage point was the bed.

Next to Katy. In her short shorts, smelling like peaches.

But if he didn't move, she'd wonder what was wrong,

which would just create a different kind of tension. Cursing his traitorous body, he willed it to behave and got up, moving to the bed to sit next to her.

Jasper did his best to keep his attention on the TV screen while they ate and ignore her presence. Once he finished eating, he got up to throw his plate away, then scooted up against the headboard, feeling himself relax a bit. She tossed her own plate, then mimicked his pose, giggling at the show.

They watched a couple episodes, chatting during commercials about what other types of television they liked to watch as well as the conference. When the third episode ended, Jasper looked over to see her eyes closed. Her chest rose and fell in a deep rhythm, and he knew she was asleep.

"Katy." He nudged her shoulder. She grumbled and turned onto her side, snuggling into the pillow.

"Dammit," he whispered. She needed to go back to her room to go to bed, but he didn't want to wake her. It might take her a while to go back to sleep, and she needed the rest.

He glanced at the door. He could go to her room and sleep and leave her here. But her key card was in her shorts pocket. If she woke up while he tried to take it from her, well, he had a feeling she might kick his ass first and ask questions second.

Picking up the remote, he turned off the TV. He got up and went into the bathroom, brushing his teeth, then wandered back out into the main room. His eyes went to the chair he sat in earlier, and he tilted his head, wondering if he'd be able to sleep there all night. It wasn't the most comfortable thing, especially for a man his size. Maybe if he sat on a pillow and stuffed another behind his back, he could do it.

He tiptoed to the bed and removed his pillows, piling them into the chair. Flipping off the lights, he made sure the alarm on his phone was set, then sank into his nest. The chair was still hard under him, but the pillows helped. Heaving a sigh, he leaned his head back and folded his hands over his abdomen, closing his eyes to the darkness in the room.

Jasper fell into a fitful sleep, not used to such a position. When Katy whimpered a few hours later, he jerked awake, staring at the bed through the darkness. She thrashed in the sheets.

"Kaz! No!"

He shot out of the chair at her shout, easing onto the bed to shake her awake. "Katy. Honey, wake up."

Her arm shot out, just missing his face. He grabbed it and tucked it against her side, then laid down behind her and wrapped her up in his arms. "Katydid, it's Jasper. You're okay." Her thrashing ebbed, but quiet sobs took their place. He shushed her and held her close. She never woke up, eventually settling into a deep sleep.

He loosened his hold, but didn't get up. She seemed more at ease with him near. Adjusting her pillows so he could lay his head on them, he closed his eyes and prayed she wouldn't kill him when she woke up to find him spooning her.

Eleven

A loud beeping drew Katy from sleep. She moaned, wishing it would stop. She stretched and yawned, then froze as the heavy weight over her middle, as well as the foreign alarm registered in her mind. Something poked her in the rear as the band around her waist shifted. She heard a distinctly male yawn behind her and jack-knifed, whirling around to see Jasper rolling over to shut off his phone alarm.

"Jasper! Why are you in my bed?"

"It's not your bed, Katydid. It's mine."

She frowned at the nickname, wondering where that came from, but was more concerned about the second part of his statement. "What do you—" she glanced around in the dim light, last evening's events playing back in her mind. "Crap. I fell asleep on your bed?"

He nodded and snapped on the bedside lamp. Her mouth went dry as she took in his sleepy appearance. Wide awake, dressed for the day, Jasper was enough to send her hormones into a tizzy. But just woke up and needs to shave Jasper? Her lady parts screamed for her to strip them both naked and sit on him while she clutched that messy hair.

She scrambled off the bed. "Why didn't you wake me up and make me go back to my room?"

"I tried. You grumbled and rolled over. I slept in the chair until you had a nightmare. Who's Kaz?"

Katy bit back a groan. She'd dreamed about Kaz? Of course she did. Because he'd invaded her dreams at least once a week lately. As tired and achy as she was yesterday, she wasn't surprised he made an appearance.

"He was my K-9," she admitted grudgingly.

"I wondered. If it's any consolation, you slept better once I calmed you down. You seemed more relaxed with me close by, so I stayed."

She found her shoes and slipped them on. "Well, thanks, I guess. Um, I'm going to go get dressed."

He nodded. "I'll meet you downstairs for breakfast in about half an hour." Tossing the covers back, he swung his legs over the bed and stood.

"M'kay." She snagged her Skittles off the dresser, then hurried from his room before he turned around and she got a glimpse of what poked her in the backside when she woke up. Even clothed, she knew it would be impressive. It had felt impressive.

She crossed the hall in one long stride, fumbling in her pocket for her key card. It tangled in the fabric of her shorts and landed on the floor. Huffing, she scooped it up, then took a deep breath, telling herself to calm down. Freaking out wouldn't help anything. It was just sleep. That's all they'd done.

Inserting the card in the slot, she let herself into her room and flipped on the lights. She didn't bother to get any clothes from her suitcase. She just turned into the bathroom and flipped on the shower. She didn't really need to bathe, but the water would help wash away the sleep and the lingering scent of Jasper on her skin. How she managed to pick that up after only a few hours—and in a bed he'd never slept in before—she didn't know. Maybe it was burned into her nostrils.

God, she hoped not. She wasn't sure she could handle smelling him all day. The man was potent.

Stepping into the hot spray, she soaped herself up, washing her hair again as well. Once all she could smell was peach body wash and shampoo, she stepped out and toweled off. Picking up her hair dryer, she dried her hair until it hung around her shoulders in sleek blonde waves, then left the bathroom to get dressed. Donning a pair of jeans, she put on a black polo shirt bearing her department's logo. She debated tying her hair back, but since she wouldn't be chasing any suspects today, she decided to leave it loose. After putting on her shoes, she filled her pockets with all the things she'd need today, then picked up the notebook she brought and left the room.

Her eyes landed on Jasper's door. She was ten minutes early. Maybe if she ate fast, she could avoid him until later. She couldn't smell him anymore, but that didn't mean she didn't remember his scent or the feel of him pressed against her.

Downstairs in the restaurant, she filled a plate with eggs, bacon, two pancakes, and some fruit, then found a seat in the back corner behind a column, hoping he didn't come looking for her.

A waitress walked up to take her drink order. Katy asked for black coffee, then poured syrup over her pancakes and dug in. Despite all the turmoil of the morning making her stomach do flips, she was hungry. She polished off her pancakes in short order, then started on her eggs.

"Why are you hiding in the corner?"

Jasper's deep voice brought her head up. He slid into the booth across from her with his plate of food.

She bit back a groan and speared some eggs. "It's just where I sat."

The server came back, bringing the coffeepot. She filled

both their mugs, then left Katy alone with him again. She shoved more eggs in her mouth, hoping she wouldn't have to talk. She didn't know what to say.

He wasn't in a talkative mood, either. Katy people-watched while she ate and tried not to notice that he hadn't bothered to shave.

Their waitress reappeared, holding the coffee carafe again. "You two want a refill?"

Katy shook her head, but Jasper held up his cup. She was wide awake thanks to Mr. Sexy across from her.

Spearing the last piece of melon on her plate, she ate it, then gulped down the rest of her coffee. Chancing a glance at Jasper, she edged toward the end of the booth. "I better get going. I want a good seat at my first seminar."

He frowned, coffee cup raised. "You still have forty-five minutes."

She shrugged and stood. "I'll mingle. See you later." With a quick smile, she fled, not waiting for a response.

Katy cursed herself as she left the restaurant. Why did that man affect her so? She'd been around handsome men before. They flocked to her like groupies. So did the not-so-handsome ones. But something about Jasper unsettled her. Left her jittery and on edge, but not in a bad way. Her body hummed around him and wanted to be closer. It was unnerving the pull he had, and she wasn't sure what to do about it.

She turned down the hallway to the conference center. A line of tables stood sentry before the double doors. Several people sat behind them, checking in attendees. Katy shoved thoughts of Jasper into the back of her mind. He could wait. She was here to learn.

TWELVE

Jasper rapped his knuckles on Katy's door, then stuffed his hands into his pockets, hoping he looked casual. Inside, he was a ball of nerves. Which was ridiculous. It was just dinner. Between friends.

Yeah, right. His conscience rolled its eyes at him. That might be what he told himself, but deep down, he knew it was more. That he wanted more. Waking up next to her—well, it felt right.

The door swung open, and need punched Jasper in the gut just like it did this morning when she looked up at him at the restaurant. She still wore her department polo, but it was untucked now.

"Hi."

He cleared his throat. "Hey. Can I come in?"

She stepped back, and he moved past her, holding his breath. If he got a whiff of that peach scent, he'd be lucky to get a coherent sentence out. Turning, he faced her as she closed the door.

"What's up?"

"I found a Moroccan place and wanted to know if you'd like to go get dinner."

"Oh." Her eyes darted around the room. "Um, I guess we could do that." She met his gaze. "Do you mind if I change first?"

He kept his eyes on her face. "Sure. Do you want me to wait in my room?" He tipped his head toward the door.

"No. You can hang out here. I'll change in the bathroom." She walked to her suitcase and dug out some clothes. "I'll be right back."

Jasper nodded, then wandered to the window. She had a better view than he did. They were downtown, and his room overlooked the road. Hers showed the city skyline.

The snick of the bathroom door opening made him turn. Katy emerged and Jasper forgot to breathe. She still wore her jeans, but she'd exchanged the black polo for a soft, drapey ombre blue sweater. It shouldn't be sexy because it was so baggy, but it was. It hinted at what she had beneath and set off that sun-kissed blonde hair of hers.

She crossed to her suitcase and laid her dirty polo on the pile next to it, then found a pair of brown leather flats in her bag and slipped them on her feet. As she straightened, he snapped out of his stupor and grabbed her jacket from the chair, holding it up.

"Oh, thanks." She turned around and slipped her arms into it.

Jasper's hands lingered a moment on her shoulders as that peach scent hit him. His nose was practically in her hair, thanks to her height. Even in her flat shoes, she was only a few inches shorter than his six-three. Swallowing hard, he stepped back and cleared his throat. "Ready?"

Her head bobbed. She picked up her purse and key card as he turned toward the door, eager to get out in the open among other people and give himself some breathing room.

"So, where is this place?" she asked as they stepped off the elevator and crossed the lobby.

He held the door open for her. "It's only a couple of blocks away, actually. I thought we could walk." He didn't know about her, but he could use the exercise after being cooped up all day. The conference was great, and he always learned something, but he was used to being on the go, not sitting in an auditorium listening to others talk.

"That sounds great."

They fell into step beside each other as they headed down the sidewalk toward the restaurant.

"So, how were your sessions?" He glanced over at her.

"They were good. I learned some great tips. I'm really looking forward to the simulation exercise on Wednesday. How about you? How was your day?"

"It was good. I brushed up on the latest technology, renewed some contacts with a few people, and prepped for my lecture tomorrow." He was slated to give his talk right after lunch.

"Nice."

"Are you coming to it?"

She nodded. "Wouldn't miss it."

He grinned, a bit of pride filling his chest. Katy was a woman who had her shit together and was excellent at her job. To be on par with her and to be able to teach her something felt nice. He'd struggled with his self-esteem for a while after he left college to take care of Megan. He'd felt a little inadequate until he finally realized his worth wasn't defined by his job, but by how well he did his job. And he was damn good at it. And at being a tracker. He'd worked hard at both, and he was proud of who he was and what he'd accomplished.

"So, a few of us were talking about having a friendly softball game tomorrow evening. You interested?"

"That sounds fun. Where are we going to play, though?"

"There are a few locals here who know the area. I guess there are ball diamonds at a local park."

"Okay, I'm game."

"You any good?"

She shrugged as they turned the corner. "I can hold my own. I get to be on your team, though, right? Going against you—well, unless the other team has a former college star, I'd rather be on your side."

He chuckled. "I think some of them played high school baseball, but that was it. I'll make sure you're on my team." He stopped in front of a building. "I think this is it."

Katy looked up at the façade and smiled. "It smells so good already."

Jasper agreed. His stomach growled as he pulled open the door and motioned her inside.

The hostess greeted them and led them to a table along the wall overlooking the street. They sat opposite each other, then gave the young woman their drink orders. She handed them each a menu and left.

"So, what's good?" He opened his menu and glanced through it.

"Depends. How spicy do you want to go?"

He shrugged. "Doesn't matter. I like it all. I think I'd rather have beef or lamb than chicken, though."

She reached over and tipped his menu down, pointing to several items on the menu. "Any of those would be good."

Jasper looked at the descriptions before deciding on the kefta tangine with poached eggs. Their server appeared with their drinks, and they gave their orders. He stuck a straw in his soda and leaned forward, propping his chin in his hand as he glanced around the colorful restaurant. His phone beeped, and he pulled it out to look at it, frowning as he saw the text from his sister.

"What's wrong?"

He glanced at Katy. "I'm not sure. It's a text from Megan. She says she's coming home, but her Easter break doesn't start until the end of the week. Would you excuse me? I want to call her."

"Of course."

Jasper slid out of the booth, already lifting the phone to his ear. It rang twice before Megan picked up.

"What's going on? Why are you coming home already? I thought you didn't get out until Friday afternoon." He went outside and away from the din of the restaurant.

Megan's sigh ended on a groan. "Yeah, but I need a break. I won't miss much, and I can turn my assignments in remotely. Burke's being a jerk."

He frowned at the mention of her boyfriend's name. Jasper didn't care for the kid. He was a cocky bastard who thought he was hot shit because he was on the school football team. Megan was always fighting with him. They'd had a big blowup while on spring break a few weeks ago. He didn't know why she was still with him. "What did he do now?"

"We went to a frat party over the weekend. I caught him flirting with some freshman—actually it was more like making out with her—he had his nose buried in her neck and his hands all over her ass. Anyway, I called him out on it. Told him I was done and left. He wouldn't stop calling me, so I blocked his number. Now he's sending me flowers and bombarding my socials. I blocked him there too."

Jasper itched to get in his truck and go give the kid a piece of his mind, but he was ten hours away. "Are you sure you can do your work from the ranch?"

"Yes. I just want to be some place he'll leave me alone. He wouldn't dare slip past Asa's security. I'd have him arrested so fast. His coach would go ape-shit if he got into trouble."

"Okay. I'll call Asa and tell him you're coming. Be careful and let me know when you're there."

"I will." She sighed again. "So, how's your conference?"

"It's a conference. I sit in a room and listen to people talk all day."

She chuckled. "Don't you have company this time, though?"

"Yeah. We're actually at dinner right now. I stepped out to call you."

"Oooh, dinner, huh? I remember Katy Lattimer. She's Mrs. Beck's granddaughter. She's gorgeous."

"Your point? She's a colleague." That he wanted her to be more was none of Megan's business.

Megan snorted. "Yeah, okay. When are you going to start living like a man in his early thirties instead of an old fuddy-duddy? I'm not a kid anymore, you know."

Jasper huffed a laugh. "I know. But my love life is none of your business. Even if we were closer in age, it still wouldn't be."

"Whatever." He could almost hear her roll her eyes at him. "It wouldn't kill you to find a girlfriend. Or a wife. You aren't getting any younger."

"Whatever," he echoed, making her laugh. "Listen, I should go. Text me when you get home, okay?"

"Okay. Have fun on your date." Her cackling rang in his ear as she hung up on him.

He couldn't stop the smile that spread over his face at her teasing. He couldn't wait to get home now. It would be nice to see her again. She was only an hour away, but with their busy lives, they only saw each other about once a month. She'd be home all week, though, for the holiday.

Shoving his phone into his front pocket, he went back into the restaurant to rejoin Katy.

"Everything okay?"

He looked up as he slid into the booth. "Yeah. Boy trouble. Her boyfriend—or I guess he's her ex-boyfriend now—is a dick. She broke up with him, and he won't leave her alone, so she's coming home a few days early to get away from him. I hope it makes him stop bugging her. If I was home, I'd be on my way to Billings to have a chat with the kid."

She arched an eyebrow. "What's he doing?"

He could see the cop wheels turning as she looked at him. "Nothing serious. Just calling and trying to get her to take him back. She said he sent flowers a couple times. Hopefully, putting some physical space between them will help him get the hint."

A small frown formed between her eyebrows, but she nodded. "Tell her to keep a record of what he does. Just in case."

His mouth flattened, but he nodded. "I don't think it'll come to anything serious. The kid's too afraid of losing his football scholarship. But I'll let her know." He sighed and sat back. "You know, when she was young, I thought I'd worry less once she could take care of herself. I don't. I just worry about different things now."

"That makes you a good parent."

His mouth pulled. "I know. And I'm not complaining about raising her. But sometimes I wish we had a normal brother-sister relationship, you know."

Katy nodded. "I know. And that might come as she gets older. Once she has a family of her own. She might see you as more of an equal then. You might too. Especially if you have young kids when she does."

"Maybe." He scratched his head with one finger and picked up his soda. "So, tell me about your brother. I'll experience a normal sibling relationship vicariously through you."

She chuckled. "What do you want to know?"

He shrugged. "Whatever you want to tell me. He's older than you, right?"

Katy nodded. "By a couple of years, yes."

"And military?"

Again, she nodded. "He's on the Ranger teams and stationed in North Carolina. His unit is deployed right now, though. In Africa."

"That's interesting. What does he do in the Rangers?"

"He's a bit of a jack of all trades, but mostly maintains their gear. He inherited Dad's mechanical abilities. Before he joined the military, he went to college and got a degree in mechanical engineering. He joined the ROTC there, then went straight into officer's school out of college. He's been a Ranger about five years now."

"What made you two go into the military?"

"Our dad. He went into the Army right out of high school. Married our mom—they were high school sweethearts —did his four-year stint to get his education paid for, then got out. He had enough knowledge working as a mechanic to get a job at the local garage while he went to night school to get certified. He owns the place now." She shrugged. "We saw what it did for our family. How it could set us up for success."

"Why an MP? Why not nursing or finance—something less deadly?"

A rueful smile crossed her face. "I've always been a tomboy. Despite my looks, I never liked the girlie-girl stuff. I was much more comfortable in cutoffs and a tank top, riding my bike at breakneck speeds behind my brother as he tried to race away from me."

Jasper chuckled at the image she painted.

"When Marcus started taking jiu jitsu lessons, I made Dad sign me up too and fell in love with it."

A frown wrinkled his forehead. "How did that lead to wanting to be military police?"

"I got to use my jiu jitsu skills on people."

He barked a laugh. She chuckled with him.

"No, that was just part of it. I took a criminal psychology

class through the college plus program at the high school and it intrigued me. But I'd known for a long time I wanted to join the Army. Becoming an MP satisfied both desires and it set me up for my future."

"So, short answer, your dad made you want to join the military?" He grinned.

She laughed. "Yeah, pretty much. So, what about you? I know how you got into ranching. But what made you get into tracking?"

He sipped his soda, his joviality leaving as he thought about what prompted him to learn some survival skills. "I got lost as a kid. Me and a buddy, Jax Lindsey. We went on a scouting trip and were working on our tracking badges. I found an elk trail, and we followed it. For quite a while, actually. Then we lost it when the ground got rocky. That's when we realized the elk wasn't the only thing we lost. We were all kinds of turned around." He shook his head and took another sip of his drink. "We didn't have a map or a compass with us. We weren't supposed to wander very far. It was just practice." He glanced away. "Once we realized the kind of trouble we were in, we started trying to figure out where we were, how long we thought we walked, which direction we went— anything that could lead us back to camp."

"And did you find it?"

"No." His voice was low, and he looked away, staring out over the restaurant at the other diners, but not seeing them. "We ended up deeper in the woods. Night fell and the temperature dropped. Then it rained. We weren't dressed properly for the weather." He could still feel the cold wet drops soaking his shirt and dripping off the ends of his hair to trickle down his face and neck. Shivers had wracked his body and all his fingers and toes turned numb and blue.

Jax's ashen, waxy face flashed through Jasper's mind. He sucked in a harsh breath and looked at Katy. "I fell asleep sometime during the night. We'd huddled together under some branches, trying to keep some of the rain off and retain some heat. When I woke up—" His voice caught, and he cleared his throat. "I couldn't wake Jax up."

Katy let out a soft gasp.

"He was still alive, but barely. I carried him to a clearing, hoping the sun would keep him warm long enough for me to build a fire."

"And did you?"

Jasper nodded. "The smoke from the fire helped the search and rescue people find us later that afternoon. But he ended up developing pneumonia a couple of days later. From mold spores that were on the leaves we used to keep us warm and off the dirt. He died a week after we got lost."

Katy's eyes went wide. "That's awful. I'm so sorry. How come you didn't get sick, though?" She frowned. "Wait. Did you?"

He shook his head. "No. Jax had asthma, so it made him more susceptible to respiratory illnesses. Any time he got even a little sniffle, he was huffing and puffing on his inhaler. And I also didn't get as cold. He was a lot smaller than me."

She reached across the table and covered his hand with hers. "I'm sorry."

He turned his hand over and gave hers a squeeze. "Thanks. Me too."

With a soft smile, she pulled her hand back. Jasper cleared his throat again, dislodging the emotion clogging it, and changed the subject. Their conversation turned to the sessions they'd attended that day and what they each learned. Jasper discovered they'd been in some of the same lectures. He wasn't sure how he missed her.

The flow of conversation ebbed when their food showed up, both of them hungry after a long day.

"So, what do you think?" Katy motioned to his plate.

He scooped up another bite of the lamb meatballs. "We need to convince Sara to put something like this on her menu."

She smiled around her fork, her head bobbing. "Or find a Moroccan restaurant willing to open a location up by us. The two of us would probably give it enough business to keep it open."

That was the truth. He'd could see himself eating something like this at least once a week. It was fantastic.

They finished their meals, declining dessert—Katy said she wanted to dive into her Skittles again later—and left the restaurant. The sun had dipped lower in the sky, casting shadows on the sidewalk. A breeze had also kicked up, adding a bite to the air. The cooler temperature wasn't unwelcome, though. The restaurant had been warm. It helped clear his head from their heavy conversation, too.

He glanced at her from the corner of his eye as they walked back to the hotel. With his mind clearing, new thoughts crept in. Would she want to go back to her room and be alone, or would she come back to his room again to watch TV like they did last night? And if she did, would they fall asleep together again?

Jasper wouldn't be sorry if that happened. She wasn't the only one who slept more soundly once he climbed into bed with her.

But as much as he enjoyed her company, he needed some space. Sitting across from her, watching her smile and laugh, all while trying to ignore the subtle scent of peaches and something unique to her waft across the table at him had worn his defenses down to practically nothing. Getting involved while they were here could create tension—negative tension—on the drive home, and then once they were back in town. Whatever blossomed between them needed to happen at a slower pace. He didn't want a fling. Megan wasn't wrong when she said he needed to get a life. He agreed. And he wanted to try to get that life with Katy. But he wanted to do it right.

Their hotel came into view. Jasper held the door open for her, then followed her into the lobby. They rode upstairs to their floor, stopping between their rooms.

"Um, I think I'm going to call it a night. I'm still tired." Katy hooked a thumb toward her door.

"Yeah. I didn't get as much sleep as I wanted either. See you at breakfast?"

She nodded. "Sure. Around seven? I'll knock when I'm ready."

"Sounds good." He hesitated, holding her gaze. His hands itched to grab her and give her a goodnight kiss. But their dinner hadn't been a date. They were just friends.

He forced his feet to move. "Goodnight, Katydid."

A corner of her mouth lifted. "Goodnight, *Jazzy*."

He laughed as he turned, "See you in the morning." He put his card in the reader and heard the snick of the lock disengaging.

"Yep."

Sending her a soft smile, he entered his room, hoping he could get thoughts of her to quiet down enough so he could sleep.

THIRTEEN

"Where did you get all this equipment?" Katy picked up a bat and a glove from the backseat of the truck, then shut the door.

"I bought it."

She paused, eyes widening. "What? Why?"

He shrugged and started toward the field, where a few others were already assembled. "We needed gloves, and I'm particular about my bat. I'm particular about my glove, too, and I wish I had mine from home, but at least this one's the same brand." He waved the glove, a bag of balls hanging beneath. "I hope yours is all right. I guessed on the size."

Katy tucked the bat under her arm and turned the mitt over in her hands, then put it on. It fit fine, even if it was a little stiff. "It's fine. Thank you. I'll pay you back."

He waved a hand. "Don't worry about it." He tossed her a quick smile. "Come on. Let's go kick some ass."

She grinned and hurried after him.

Once everyone arrived, they gathered near one of the dugouts to split into teams.

"We need two team captains," one of the men said.

"I vote for John to be one." Jasper pointed to a middle-aged man with dirty blonde hair and an easy smile. "This was your idea, after all."

John shrugged. "Sure. So long as you're the other one." He flashed a grin. "I want to see if I can kick Mr. All-State's booty."

"It's actually Mr. National Team, but we won't argue semantics." Jasper chuckled.

John laughed. "I stand corrected. It will only make victory sweeter, though."

"Sure." He grinned, then looked over the group. "Are we in agreement?"

They all nodded.

"Good, then let's pick teams. Go ahead, John."

The other man shook his head. "You're my guest. You start."

"You sure?"

He nodded. "Absolutely."

"Okay." He looked at Katy. "I'll take Katy."

John picked a local friend of his. They traded choices until they each had seven players. Their outfield would be spread thin, but it was doable.

"You ready to flip for home team?" John took a quarter from his pocket.

Jasper waved a hand. "You take it." A wide smile spread over his face. "You're going to need the advantage."

"Oh, cocky much?" John stuffed the quarter back into his pocket as they all laughed. "I'm not arguing, though." He glanced at his team. "Come on, guys. Let's go kick some Montana butt." They ran out onto the field.

Jasper motioned his team closer. Someone produced a notebook, and after asking a few questions about experience levels, he wrote out a quick batting order, putting himself third. Katy was fifth. She couldn't help but marvel at how confident he seemed in his role as coach and wondered why he wasn't involved with their local high school team. She made a mental note to ask later.

Their lead-off hitter, Mike, stepped to the plate. John designated himself as pitcher and the game started. After hitting a ground ball past the shortstop, Mike stopped at first base. The next hitter hit a pop-fly that was caught by the third baseman at the edge of the grass. Then it was Jasper's turn. He handed Katy the notebook, then grabbed his bat.

From the moment he stepped into the batter's box, she could tell he was a different kind of player. That bat was a natural extension of his arms. Anticipation built in her stomach.

John gave him some good-natured ribbing, then tossed the ball. It floated toward Jasper, sailing over his head.

"Really?" Jasper straightened and gave him a look. "You that scared of me you have to walk me?"

"No." John grinned. "It slipped."

"Sure it did." Jasper took his stance again, a smile quirking his mouth. "Give me a good one."

Laughing, John lobbed another pitch. This one came right down the middle. Katy held her breath.

The bat pinged as he connected with the ball. It sailed over everyone's heads and over the fence.

Katy whooped as he took off around the bases.

"Oh, it's on!" John yelled.

Jasper laughed and rounded third. His long legs ate up the ground to home plate. Katy met him with a smile.

"That was amazing! I just have one question, though?"

He grinned as he took the notebook back from her. "What's that?"

"Who's going to go get that ball?"

She joined in his laughter as it echoed over the field.

FOURTEEN

"I'm a sweaty mess."

Jasper glanced over as Katy pulled her t-shirt away from her body and fanned herself with it. They were on their way to the truck after the game.

"Me too. How's your leg?" He hadn't seen her limping or rubbing it, but she hid pain well, he'd noticed.

"It's fine. No more achy than usual."

"That's good. So, no hot tub, then?"

A smile tilted one corner of her mouth. "Well, I didn't say that." She pulled on the passenger door handle and climbed in.

Jasper got in beside her, depositing his gear in the backseat. His heart thumped a little faster at the thought of seeing her in a swimsuit again. He wondered if she'd wear a bikini if they were at the beach.

He stifled a groan as that image hit him. That was a thought better left for when he was alone. Starting the truck, he pulled out of the parking lot.

"That was fun," Katy said. "I'm glad your friend arranged it. Though, I don't think he is." She gave a soft chuckle.

Jasper laughed. "Yeah. I don't think he believed me when I told him if it hadn't been for my mom dying, I'd have gone pro. He does now."

"I'd say so, yes. Why don't you coach the high school team? You're really good at it. Coaching, I mean. Not just the game."

He sighed and rested his wrist over the steering wheel as he drove, his other arm propped on the windowsill. "At first, it hurt too much to even play the game. I'd had so many dreams, you know? I didn't regret stepping away. Megan was more important than any game. But it was still disappointing to give up the idea of going pro. Since then, I guess it's never really come up. I put baseball in my past, and that's where it's stayed."

"Hmm. Well, I think you should look into coaching. Kids could learn a lot from you. Even if you volunteer at first. My department works with the schools, and I know the coaches. I can talk to them for you."

He ran a finger over his upper lip, considering her proposal. "Honestly, I'm not sure how I feel about getting back into. I'll think about it, though."

"Good enough for me." She smiled and sat back, closing her eyes against the breeze that came in through her window.

They arrived at the hotel and went upstairs, agreeing to meet at the pool in ten minutes. Jasper changed and headed down, stopping to get them each a water and a pack of Skittles. He entered the poolroom, astonished to find it empty. Setting his stuff down on a chair, he toed off his shoes and took off his shirt, intending to take full advantage of the lack of swimmers.

He walked down the stairs and started swimming. The pool wasn't large, so he reached the other side in a few strokes, but it felt good to stretch his muscles after the game. When he got back to the ranch, he needed to talk Asa into putting in a pool. It would be good therapy for all of them. Not to mention fun.

"Do you even use a tenth of your breath in one lap?"

Jasper paused at the edge and looked up, swiping water from his eyes. Katy stood above him, one eyebrow quirked. He grinned. "Not really, no. But it's still nice to swim."

She turned away, walking to the chairs and giving him a prime view of her firm butt as she took off her shorts and shirt. As she came back, he couldn't help but note that the front of her was just as good. She sat down on the pool deck and put her feet in the water. He moved in front of her, sliding in between her legs.

That eyebrow went up again. "You going to move so I can get in?"

"Thought I'd help." His smile widened. Before she could react, he grasped her waist and lifted, turning toward the deeper water, then tossed her. She landed with a splash.

Sputtering as she broke the surface, she wiped water from her eyes. "Oh! Oh, you're dead." Laughing, she dove at him. Her arms went around his shoulders and her legs around his waist, pushing on his head. But they were in the middle of the pool, and his six-foot-three-inch height meant he could stand flat-footed and still have his shoulders above water.

He wrapped his arms around her and fell sideways, then pushed her away and came up, grinning. "You realize I'm bigger and stronger than you, right?"

She splashed him, and he lunged for her, keeping them above the water this time.

"Let go." She pushed at his shoulders, giggling.

His deep laughter joined hers. "No way. You're tenacious. I'll turn my back and get splashed again."

A wicked grin slashed across her face. She quit trying to shove her way out of his arms and slapped her hands on the water, sending up a spray into his face. Jasper pinned her hands down, squeezing her body to his. "Minx."

She squirmed, then huffed. "If we were on dry ground, I'd drop you."

His low chuckle echoed off the water. "I know you would."

The sour glare she sent up at him through her lashes only made him chuckle more. She smiled, then, and relaxed into his embrace. A slow heat built in his belly and his playfulness turned to something more.

Her pupils dilated and her breathing changed. When she pulled at her arms, he let them go. But rather than move away, she raised her hands to his shoulders, staying close. He raised a hand to the side of her neck, keeping the other at her waist.

She tucked herself closer, raising up. Everything faded around him except the feel of the woman in his arms. His eyes dropped to her mouth, which parted as he leaned closer. He caught her gaze again. The same heat he felt burning in his blood stared back at him from her eyes. Closing the distance, he kissed her.

FIFTEEN

What the hell am I doing?

The thought reverberated through Katy's mind as she kissed Jasper back, but she didn't pull away. She couldn't. He had her enthralled with a simple kiss.

She'd wondered what it would feel like, but her imagination had left her woefully unprepared. There were sparks, which she anticipated, but not this lightning storm that went off behind her eyelids. Or the raging wildfire sweeping through her body.

The heat engulfed them both. He tightened his arm around her and deepened the kiss. She moaned against him and nipped at his lower lip. His responding growl sent a delicious shiver down her spine. She raised her legs and wrapped them around his waist. His hot length pressed against her core, and she let out a soft whimper.

Voices intruded through the desire clouding her brain. She lifted her head, staring down at him. His chest heaved beneath her hands. Those gray eyes of his were a steely blue as he held her gaze.

Katy bit her lip and unwrapped her legs. Two kids jumped

into the pool. She felt the drops from the splash they sent up hit her face. It brought her mind into focus, and she glanced away, swallowing hard.

What was that? Where did that come from?

With a quick look at him, she sank beneath the water and swam away, leaving him there standing as rigid as a statue. Resurfacing near the edge, she pulled herself from the water and walked straight to the hot tub. Jasper stayed in the pool, wading into deeper water away from the kids.

She watched him, her mind whirling as she tried to process the sudden turn her life just took. There was no going back to pretending they were just friends. Not after a kiss like that. She wasn't entirely sure what would have happened if those kids hadn't come in. Would they have gone upstairs to one of their rooms?

Hell, she wanted to do that now. But she didn't jump into bed with a man outside of a committed relationship. They hadn't committed to anything except being friends.

Katy sighed and leaned her head back, closing her eyes. What a mess.

Water sloshed around her, and she clenched her teeth together, steeling herself against having Jasper close enough to touch. She opened her eyes, surprise making them wide as she saw it wasn't Jasper, but the man that hit on her the other day.

He smiled politely and settled against the opposite side. She returned his smile and closed her eyes again, praying he'd leave her alone this time.

"You have a fight with your boyfriend?"

Katy's chest heaved as she sighed. She just wanted to relax. "No."

"Then how come he looks like he wants to pound on something, and you look like you could rip someone's innards out and stomp on them?"

Surprise at his words drew a short laugh from her. She looked at him. "Rip out someone's innards?"

He shrugged, his smile sheepish.

She gave him a more genuine smile. "We're not fighting. It's just been a busy day." She didn't bother denying Jasper was her boyfriend. The last thing she wanted was for this man to take that as an invitation. Even if she were into picking up random men, her body only wanted one in particular.

Her gaze went to Jasper as he heaved himself from the pool. Water cascaded over his well-defined muscles. It was like watching one of those perfume commercials where the guy walked out of the ocean. Only Jasper wasn't behind some screen.

She felt her nipples peak and sank lower into the water. He rounded the perimeter of the pool to come her way. Tipping her head back, she looked up at him, doing her damnedest to ignore the way his trunks hugged everything south of his waist.

"You ready to go, Katydid? It's getting late and we have an early morning."

A small thrill went through her at the nickname. While she didn't understand the comparison to a grasshopper, she couldn't deny the fact she liked that he'd given her a pet name. And that it was different from the one her parents and brother used. They called her Katy-bug.

She nodded and stood, climbing the steps out of the hot tub. Following him to the chairs where they left their stuff, she dried off, then wrapped the towel around herself and put on her shoes. Jasper put on his shirt and shoes, then they gathered the rest of their things and left.

The ride up to their floor was a quiet one. She stared straight ahead at the doors, arms tucked close as she clutched her clothes. When the elevator dinged and the doors parted, she shot out of the car and down the hall. Her door came into view, and her feet carried her just a little faster. She found her key card, ready to escape temptation.

"Katy."

So close! She paused in front of her door and glanced back.

"Are we going to talk about what happened?"

She rolled her bottom lip in and looked at the floor. "Do we need to?" Because she really didn't want to. She preferred to ignore it for now. Until she could process it. That would take at least a bag of Skittles and a few hours alone.

He stepped closer, and she looked up. Her breath caught in her throat as he neared.

"Yes. What happened—well, it happened, and we need to figure out what we're going to do about it. I can't just ignore it. Can you?"

Totally. But not without creating some unbearable tension. And not the good kind. Her mouth flattened, and she shook her head. "Can we agree to table the discussion?"

He frowned. She could see a protest growing in his eyes, and held out a hand.

"Not forever. Just until we get home. Right now, can we agree to acknowledge that something happened and leave it at that? I want to concentrate on tomorrow's exercise with a clear head. If we—muddle things up anymore, I'll end up thinking about that when I should be thinking about the rescue operation."

His expression cleared. "All right." He nodded. "Until we get home."

Katy gave him a soft smile, grateful he'd agreed. "Thanks." She angled her body toward the door. "I guess I'll see you in the morning."

"Yep. Breakfast at five. We need to be at the site by six." He backed toward his room.

"Sounds good. Goodnight, Jasper."

"Goodnight, Katydid."

Sixteen

Katy lifted the radio mic to her mouth and gave instructions to one of the teams she was managing in the field. The biggest draw to this conference for her was the opportunity for real-world, practical experience in a simulated exercise. Somewhere out there in the Utah desert was a bright green flag with her section number on it. It was her responsibility to keep track of her teams and relay information to them while coordinating with the other law enforcement and the press. The latter two were volunteers pretending to be those agencies, but her efforts were real.

So far, things were going great. She'd been a little overwhelmed at first when the instructor gave her the rundown, then pointed her to her station. There was just so much information to assimilate. But once she got a handle on the reports and looked at the map, she was able to put into practice the things she'd learned the last couple of days.

"Who's got sector four?" The instructor's voice carried over the area where they were set up.

Katy held up a hand, not taking her eyes off the map on her whiteboard as one of her teams radioed in that their current quadrant was clear and they were moving on to the next. With a grease pencil, she put hash marks over the laminated document for their sector as the instructor walked up.

"What's the position of all your teams?"

She pointed to the map, where small blue magnets denoted the location of each team. He studied it, a different kind of tension lining his shoulders.

"Gary, is everything okay?"

He shook his head. "We just got a report of a child who wandered away from his parents. They went off the trail to explore and got turned around. The kid wandered off while the parents tried to pinpoint their location on a map. They searched their immediate vicinity, but couldn't find him. The dad got to high ground and called for help. I'm pulling the other search teams to your quadrant. You have Jasper Hendriks already, right?"

Her heart beat faster. "Yes."

"Get him on the radio and tell him to proceed to these coordinates and rendezvous with the parents." He wrote a series of numbers on the whiteboard.

She lifted the radio, then hesitated. "This is for real, right? Not some twist you're throwing in to test my ability to adapt?"

"No, it's for real. Though that's not a bad idea." He pointed at the radio. "Call Jasper."

Tamping down the adrenaline that wanted to flood her system at this turn of events, she nodded. "Do you have any info on the boy? Name, age, disabilities, what he was wearing?"

"Kid's name is Dylan Shumaker. He's five. Blonde. I don't know about disabilities, but he was wearing jean shorts and a white t-shirt with a dinosaur on it.

"Okay." She pressed the mic button. "Base to tracker team one."

"Tracker team one, go ahead."

Hearing Jasper's voice helped to further calm her nerves. With him in the field, they had a better-than-average chance of finding that kid sooner rather than later. "Jasper, I need you to go to the following coordinates." She read the coordinates from the board. "This is no longer an exercise. We've received a report of a lost child. Dylan Shumaker. Five-year-old male. Blonde hair, wearing jean shorts and a white t-shirt with a dinosaur on it. His parents are waiting for you at that location."

A beat of silence passed. She could picture his face as that information registered. It'd be blank for a moment before a fierce, determined frown would take over. He was also likely muttering several curses in his head.

"Copy base. Proceeding to coordinates. Tracker team one out."

Katy turned back to Gary. "How long has he been missing?"

"An hour."

She grimaced, then nodded and looked at her map. "The average walking speed of a child that age is about two and a half to three miles per hour, so we can assume a search zone about like this." She used the marker and a ruler to plot points on the map, then connected them with a circle.

Gary stepped closer to examine her work. "He likely didn't walk linearly, so that's a good area to start with. Tell your teams on the fringe to start a quadrant search as they work their way to the middle. It's unconventional, but we'll lose time if they hike all the way to the middle and then back out. Just make sure they're diligent about radioing in once they clear a sector. And mark those sectors with a different color. I want you to send a sweep out from his last known position, and we'll cover those areas again, just to be sure he didn't wander into one of them after the team passed through."

She nodded, then relayed the information to her teams coming in.

"I called in a chopper. I don't know how much luck we'll have, because he's an awful small target, but it's worth a shot. I'm hoping that white shirt of his will pop against all that red rock."

So did she. Tapping the marker against her hand, she continued to coordinate the efforts, adding the other groups to her map as Gary called them to the area. She itched to be out there searching, but knew that right now, this was where she was needed. There were plenty of capable individuals—including Jasper—out there looking for the boy.

SEVENTEEN

Long legs eating up the ground, Jasper led his small team of three other individuals, which included his friend John, who was a medic, and two other searchers, Trina and Joel, up the steep grade to where the parents waited. As they crested the hill, he saw the mother sitting on the ground, her head pressed against her raised knees and the father pacing nearby.

The man spotted them and hurried over. His wife looked up at the quick shuffle of his feet and stood.

"Are you from search and rescue?"

Jasper nodded and extended a hand to the dad. "Jasper Hendriks." He quickly introduced the rest of the team.

"Allan Shumaker. This is my wife, Melinda." Allan shook his hand. "Is there any word?"

"Not yet, but we've just started searching. Can you take me to the spot you last saw him?"

The man nodded, but frowned. "Don't we need to wait for the others?"

He shook his head. "They'll get direction from base. My

job is to follow your son's trail, but I need you to show me where it starts."

"Oh, okay." The man turned, nudging his wife down the hill.

Jasper and his team followed them into the canyon. A breeze whipped through the trench. Tracking the child through this terrain would not be easy.

"This is where we were." Melinda said. "We got turned around, so we got the compass out and the map. We'd just decided to climb the hill when I turned around and he was gone. It couldn't have been more than a minute or so." Her face crumpled. "I don't know why he would have wandered off. We hike all the time. He's never done anything like this before."

"Does your son have any disabilities? Autism or any other developmental disorders?"

She shook her head. "No. That's why this doesn't make sense. He knows better."

Jasper bit the corner of his mouth and nodded. His attention was already on the ground. "You were standing there." He pointed to a spot to his right, then turned. "And he was there." He pointed in front of him. Walking closer, he saw the telltale scuffs made by the boy's shoes.

"We searched several of the paths, but once we didn't find him after a few hundred feet in each direction, we turned back. We didn't want to go down the wrong one and get too far away," Allan said.

He was glad the parents kept their wits about them. He could be out here searching for three people instead of one.

Eyes on the ground, Jasper followed the scuffs, pausing several times to examine some spots more closely. He heard a chopper inbound and hoped they could spot the boy from the air. The day was mild, but the kid still didn't have any water, and there were other dangers in the desert besides dehydration.

He tamped down the heightened sense of urgency he always got when searching for missing children. Jasper learned a long time ago that the extra adrenaline didn't help him focus, and he ended up making mistakes.

The radio squawked on occasion as they walked, the other teams on the ground and in the air relaying completed search quadrants. Jasper called in his location and asked for the chopper to circle outward from his position. He was definitely on the kid's trail. Having the chopper overhead would be useful.

An hour later, and two and a half hours after the boy went missing, the chopper spotted him three hundred yards down the canyon from Jasper's position. It hovered overhead while he and his team, along with the boy's parents, hurried to him.

"Dylan!" Melinda cried out when she saw him.

"Mommy!" The boy ran forward into his mother's arms.

"Oh! My baby!" She scooped him up. Allan dropped next to her and wrapped his arms around them both.

Jasper blew out a breath, relieved they found him. He lifted his radio. "Tracker team one to base. We found the boy. He's fine. Over."

"Tracker one, that's great. I'll instruct the pilot to land on the hill and bring the Shumakers back to base. Over."

"Sounds good. See you soon. Tracker team one, out."

He walked up to the reunited family in time to hear Allan ask Dylan why he wandered away.

"I saw a lizard and followed it, but I didn't pay attention to where I was going. And then I couldn't see you and everything looked the same." Tears welled in the boy's eyes and his voice wavered.

"Why didn't you stay put and let us find you?"

"I wanted to get up the hill so you could see me." He sniffed. "But then I couldn't find the right path."

Jasper crouched in front of the boy. "Hi, Dylan. My name's Jasper."

The boy sniffed again and wiped his nose on his arm. "Hi."

"You okay?"

Dylan nodded.

"Anything bite you or sting you?"

"Mosquitoes."

Jasper smiled and ruffled the boy's blonde hair. "Good deal. You're going to be just fine. If you ever find yourself lost again, just stay put, okay? Unless the place you're in isn't safe. Otherwise, hunker down and let your parents find you."

He nodded again. "Okay. I'm sorry."

"Don't be sorry. You didn't mean to get lost." Jasper stood. "Come on. There's a chopper waiting to take you back to our base."

The kid's eyes widened. "I get to ride in a helicopter?" Awe wiped away any trace of tears.

Jasper tried to keep his expression stern, but the corners of his mouth lifted. "Yes. But that's not an excuse to get lost in the future."

Dylan giggled. "I won't, I swear."

"Good." Jasper let his smile free. "Let's go."

Eighteen

Katy arched her back, pressing her fist into her lower spine. Being on her feet all day, not walking much, always made it ache. She could go for another dip in the hot tub, but unless Jasper stayed in his room, she wasn't going anywhere near it. She'd fill up her bathtub and soak in private tonight.

Rotor blades made a steady whump-whump in the air as the chopper left. It had dropped off its passengers, and the pilot had made his report to the incident commander, which was actually the local sheriff. Because they'd already been up here conducting their exercise, he had left the running of the operation up to her.

"You did good, kid."

She glanced up at Gary, wrinkling her nose at the moniker. To him, though, she was. The man had to be close to seventy. "Thanks. It was a team effort."

He nodded. "And you had a good one." He took down the map after wiping it clean and rolled it up.

"I'm just glad we were already out here. If the kid had to get lost, here, today, was a good time to do it."

He snickered. "That's for sure."

Movement out of the corner of her eye drew her attention. She looked over to see Jasper appear at the trailhead with his team. That little thrill he evoked ran up her spine. She shook off the shiver and went back to cleaning up her workstation. Apparently, time apart did little to diminish the effect he had on her.

"Jasper." Gary stepped away to greet him. "Good work out there."

"Thanks."

Katy glanced over to see him shake Gary's hand. His eyes met hers. She offered him a quick smile, then went back to packing up.

"Need help?"

She looked up again. "Oh, no. I'm fine. Go sit down and take a break. You could use one after all that hiking, I'm guessing." She gathered a stack of papers and shoved them in a folder.

He took it from her. "So could you. You're standing funny. What hurts? Your back or your leg? Or both?"

Her mouth twisted. When did he get so good at reading her body language? "I'm fine."

"I don't believe you, so how about you tell me what needs to be done so we can both go take a break?"

She huffed. "Fine. We just need to finish clearing my station and load the stuff into Gary's truck."

"Okay. Let me put my pack in our truck, then I'll start carrying things to his." He spun away before she could protest further.

Grumbling to herself about stubborn men, she stuffed things into a crate. He returned a few minutes later and picked up the crate and radio. She turned the table on its side and collapsed the legs, folding it up and latching it. She straightened, wincing. That bath couldn't happen soon enough. Her muscles were getting tighter and tighter.

Jasper reappeared and picked up the table. "Say your goodbyes. I'm going to put this away, then bring the truck around, so we can go."

The look in his eyes told her he'd seen her wince. She wasn't going to argue, though. Not when it meant she got to get her bath.

She found Gary at one of the other workstations, thanking him for the seminar and for his guidance. He wished her luck, and she headed for the parking lot, reaching it as Jasper pulled up to the curb.

Katy didn't bother to hide her sigh as her butt hit the seat. It felt nice to sit.

"How bad is it?"

She latched her seatbelt and looked at him. "How bad is what?"

"Your back." He put the truck in gear and drove out of the lot.

Blowing out a breath, she shifted, then pushed the button on the side of the seat that increased her lumbar support. "It's not that bad. Stop worrying about me. A backache is nothing new after a long day, Jasper."

He frowned. "Can't your doctors do anything about it?"

She shook her head. "No. It's as good as it's going to get." She rested her elbow on the windowsill, putting her chin in her hand as she looked out at the passing scenery. "I'm lucky I can walk."

Silence filled the vehicle. She glanced over to see a muscle twitch in his jaw.

"Are you ready to tell me what happened?"

That clammy feeling she got every time she thought about what happened to her crawled over her skin. She suppressed a shudder and shook her head. "No."

"Have you thought about what I said? About sharing the pain?"

It had been on her mind, but like her relationship with him, she refused to give it too much brain power yet. "A bit. I know I need to deal with it. And I will. But not today."

The rest of their ride back to the city was quiet. Jasper turned on the radio and a content, if not entirely comfortable silence fell between them. They were both too tired to deal with their feelings for each other. Especially when they were headed home tomorrow and would be stuck in a confined space with each other all day. She needed to mentally prepare herself for that occurrence.

Upstairs, she paused outside her door. "Hey, if you don't mind, I think I'm going to order room service tonight. I want to soak in the tub and go to bed early."

"Sounds good. I'd like to be on the road by six or so."

"Okay."

His head bobbed once. "See you in the morning." Inserting his key card in his door, he pushed into his room, shoulders stiff.

She sighed and let herself into her room. She didn't know if she'd upset him or if he was just as tired as she was. It was likely a combination of both.

Katy dropped her bag on the floor and sat down in the chair at the desk to look at the room service menu. She wanted junk food. Comfort food. Reaching for the phone, she called the number listed and placed an order for grilled cheese, fries, a large water, and a piece of cheesecake.

While she waited, she dug out the bubble bath she never went anywhere without, her pajamas, and a book and took them into the bathroom. She wanted to hop into the bath as soon as she finished eating.

Once she had everything ready, she opened her laptop and logged into the hotel's wifi, so she could check her work email.

So far, there hadn't been any fires to put out. Ray was handling the day-to-day and forwarding her anything that needed her attention. It was all administrative stuff that made her eyes cross and gave her a headache.

When the hotel employee knocked on her door with her food thirty minutes later, she was glad for the reprieve. She tipped the young woman who brought her tray, then sat down at the desk to eat while she finished going through her email. She clicked send on her last reply as she finished her cheesecake.

Cleaning up her mess, she set the empty tray in the hallway, then walked into the bathroom. As the tub filled, she stripped out of her clothes. The large mirror showed her reflection as she turned. The scars crisscrossing her lower back shone silver in the harsh light.

A lump formed in her chest, and she leaned on the counter, staring at herself. Her physical scars had faded over the years, but her internal ones still bled from time to time. Especially when she felt vulnerable. They pushed against her boundaries, then, knowing they were weak.

Like this past week. Jasper had created cracks in all her walls, not just the ones to her heart. He demanded everything of her—and rightly so—if they were to ever have anything other than friendship. It just unnerved her that her mind let him when they hadn't even talked about what, if anything, they were going to do about their feelings for each other.

She turned away, shoving thoughts of her past firmly behind a locked door. She'd meant it when she said she wasn't ready to deal with them today.

Steam filled the bathroom, along with the comforting scent of her peach bubble bath. She stepped over the edge with her book and sank into the sea of bubbles. The pain in her back disappeared as she relaxed in the garden tub. She needed to remember this hotel chain when she traveled next. The tub was fantastic. Almost as good as the hot tub.

Sighing as some of the tension left her body, she opened her book, determined to lose herself in the pages of her fantasy novel.

Nineteen

Jasper bit back a yawn as he stood by his truck in the pre-dawn light, waiting for Katy. They'd finished breakfast, and she'd wanted to use the restroom before they left. He'd brought their bags out while he waited.

Another yawn cracked his jaw. He didn't know why he thought such an early start time was a good thing.

The front doors swished open and Katy walked out, looking fresh and rested. He was glad one of them got some sleep, at least. He'd tossed and turned most of the night, first imagining her naked in a bathtub full of bubbles, then wondering why she wanted to keep him at arm's length and how he could fix that. He still didn't have any answers.

She smiled as she neared and held out a cup of coffee. "You looked like you needed this for the road."

He took the steaming cup, moaning as the scent hit his nose. "Oh, yes. Thanks."

"You're welcome."

Jasper took a sip of the coffee as they got in the truck. "Are we ready to go?"

"Yep." She buckled her seatbelt, then picked up her coffee again.

He took another drink of his, then started the car and pointed them toward the highway. He drove for nearly half an hour before he felt awake enough to hold a conversation. Katy must have felt the same, because she stared out the window.

"So, do you want to stop anywhere on the way home? We didn't do much sightseeing."

"Like where?"

"Um..." He scratched his temple. "Lava Springs is on the way. So is Yellowstone." He frowned. "But I think it's still closed to most automobile traffic."

"I've had enough of the great outdoors for a bit. Unless it's a beach. Can we detour to the beach?"

He chuckled. Sun and sand did sound nice. "Not in a day, unfortunately. But maybe we should plan something like that for this summer." He chanced a look at her. She'd stiffened.

Jasper sighed. "Katy, I think we need to talk about us. I know we're not home yet, but we're also not at the conference anymore."

"Jasper—"

He held up a hand. "I'm not asking for a lifetime commitment." He looked at her. "I just want to know if I asked you on a date, would you say yes?"

She stared at him for a beat. "Are you asking?"

His jaw worked. "Yes." He sent another glance her way. "Will you go on a date with me when we get home?"

She sucked in that lower lip, working it between her teeth. Jasper stole glances at her while he watched the road and she considered his question.

"Okay."

"Okay?" Hope sparked in his chest.

"Yeah." She nodded. "I'll go on a date with you. I can't deny I'm attracted to you. You wouldn't believe me if I did.

And I don't want to deny it. It's just—" She broke off with a sigh.

"Just what?"

Her mouth flattened, then she looked at her hands, picking at her nails before she glanced back up at him. "I don't want to shortchange you. Us."

He frowned. "How would you do that?"

"Because of my job. I'm always on call. I work stupidly long hours. I barely have enough time for me, let alone someone else. I don't want you to feel like I neglect you."

Jasper put his elbow on the windowsill and propped his jaw in his hand. He hadn't given that aspect of things much thought. "I think it'll be an adjustment for both of us. I understand you have a demanding job." He reached over and covered her hands. "I just want to spend time with you. In case you haven't noticed, I kinda think you're great."

A blush stole over her face, accompanied by a soft smile. "You aren't so bad yourself."

He grinned. "So, we're going to give this a try?"

She blew out a breath. "Yeah. Okay. But please be patient with me? My life is organized chaos. Mostly. Other times, it's not organized at all."

Jasper chuckled and threaded his fingers through hers, some of the tension leaving his shoulders now that they'd cleared the air between them. "You got it."

Twenty

Katy stared through the windshield at her house as Jasper pulled into her driveway and put the truck in park, then cut the engine. Silence filled the cab. She wasn't sure how to say goodbye. Did she just get out and go inside? Did they make plans for their date? Should she invite him inside?

She bit back a frustrated moan. This was part of why she didn't date. She never knew how to act or what to say.

"So... we're here." Jasper took off his seatbelt.

"Yep." She unfastened hers and got out, rolling her eyes at herself. That was such a witty comeback. Why did agreeing to see him romantically take away her ability to act like an intelligent adult? She opened the back door and removed her suitcase and duffel, then leaned in to grab her purse. Turning, she let out a small squeak of surprise. Jasper stood in front of her.

"Don't do that!" She smacked his chest. The man moved like the wind. She didn't even hear his door shut. Though that was probably more because she was stuck in her own head than his ninja skills. Mentally, she rolled her eyes. Some cop she was. It's a good thing he wasn't out to do her harm.

She reached for her suitcase, but he pulled the handle back.

"I've got it."

"Oh. That's okay. I can get it."

"I know. Doesn't mean I'm going to let you carry your own bags."

She arched an eyebrow. "You let me carry them downstairs at the hotel."

"One, my hands were full already, and two, you were like a blonde-haired runaway locomotive. Those elevator doors opened and you were gone." He smiled.

Her mouth twitched at the imagery. "So, what you're saying is I should have been faster about getting my things from the truck?"

"Yes."

A laugh slid free. "Fine." She stepped around him, leading him to her front door. Finding her keys in her purse, she let them inside, flipping on the lights as she entered. "You can just leave them there in the entryway. I'll take them upstairs later."

He set the suitcase against the wall just past the entry table and put her duffel on top. Katy put her keys and purse on the table, then turned to face him.

"Well." She wrung her hands together, feeling awkward again. "Um, thanks for bringing my stuff in. And for driving. You'll have to let me know what I owe you for gas."

"I will." He stepped closer.

The fine hairs on her neck and arms stood up. "Jasper?"

He took her face in his hands. Startled, she grasped his wrists and met his gaze. It burned that same steely blue as when they kissed in the pool. Her stomach flip-flopped, and her eyelids fluttered closed as he leaned in.

Soft lips pressed to her cheekbone beneath her left eye, then they were gone, along with his hands. She opened her eyes to see that he'd taken a step back, but the heat was still there in his gaze.

"I'm going to go before we move faster than either of us is ready for."

Katy sucked in a breath, steadying the wild beat of her heart, and nodded. "Okay."

He backed toward the door. "I'll call you soon, and we'll plan that date." With a smile and a wink, he turned and let himself out.

All the starch left her muscles. She took two steps toward the wall and sagged against it. Holy hell. He'd barely touched her and her entire body hummed. It was probably a good thing he hadn't kissed her again. Even knowing she wasn't ready for more, she might not have cared.

Twenty-One

"Katrina? Are you home, dear?"

Katy looked over the back of the couch as her grandma came through the front door carrying a large box. "Grandma." She put her half-eaten dinner on the coffee table and got up, hurrying around to help. "What is this?"

Heidi handed over the box and closed the door. "Costumes. I was hoping to get your opinion."

"Oh?" It had been years since she helped with costumes. "What's this for?" Heidi had retired two years ago, so this couldn't be for a book she was teaching to her students.

"I offered to help with the school musical. They're doing 'Zombie Prom.'"

"Zombie what?" She carried the box into the living room and set it on one end of the couch.

"Prom. It's set in the fifties, and it's about a high school couple who are dating. The girl's father disapproves and makes her dump her boyfriend. The boy, so distraught over the breakup, crawls into a radioactive waste dump and dies. He reappears later as a zombie who just wants to be a normal kid, but the principal doesn't want to let a zombie into the school. I read the script. It's going to be great." Heidi paused as she reached for the box, her eyes on the plate Katy had left on the table. "Did I interrupt your dinner?"

"Huh? Oh, yes, but I can finish it while you show me what's in the box."

"You sure?"

Katy nodded. "Yes. I want to see these costumes."

Heidi opened the box. "So, since it's set in the fifties, I went with poodle-style skirts, but without the poodles." She pulled out several floral print and pastel skirts. "They're all wraps." She unfastened the tab closure on one and pulled it open into a long panel. "That way, they'll fit anyone."

"Okay. What about tops?"

"I was going to tell the girls to wear either a short-sleeved, solid color button-up or a sweater set to match their skirt."

"That sounds good."

"Great. For the boys, I was going to look for or make some dark wash straight-leg jeans. They can wear a solid or striped tee, then. And I know I can get some plain vintage jackets at the thrift stores in Billings. What I really want your opinion on, though, is the zombie costume for the Jonny Warner character." She pulled a pair of acid wash jeans and a black t-shirt, both full of holes, from the box.

"That's it?" Katy frowned at the clothes. "Where's the gore? He's a frickin' zombie."

Heidi rolled her eyes. "Yes, but it's also a high school musical." She reached into the box again, removing a faux leather jacket with bleach and burn marks and one sleeve missing. "On the exposed arm, we were going to put some raw patches. He'll have wounds on his face too. That's about as gory as the principal would let me go. There will be little kids in the audience, so we couldn't do scary. He's a friendly zombie, anyway."

Katy chuckled. "I guess that makes sense. When are they putting this on? I think I'd like to go."

"End of the school year. Which is perfect. I need to concentrate on Easter. Oh! Speaking of, do you know of anyone who'd be willing to play the Easter Bunny for the church egg hunt? It'd just be for a few hours the day before."

Katy frowned at the abrupt change of subject. "No one's coming to mind off the top of my head, but I can ask around at work. Maybe Ray will do it. His mom is pretty involved in all of that stuff, isn't she?"

Heidi's nose wrinkled. "She already asked and got a resounding no."

That didn't surprise Katy. He was quite an introvert. A good cop, but an introvert.

"What about that friend of yours? The one you went to Salt Lake City with. Jasper?"

Katy narrowed her eyes, noting the mischief lighting her grandma's face. "Grandma." She drew out the word, a note of warning in her tone. She knew something was suspicious about the sudden change of subject.

Heidi grinned and shrugged one shoulder. "What? I just asked a simple question."

"Sure you did."

"So? Do you think he would play the Easter Bunny?"

"I don't think he'd fit in the costume, Grandma."

"They make them for tall people."

"Where would he find an extra-tall Easter Bunny costume the weekend before Easter?"

Heidi's mouth turned down. "Damn. Good point." Her face brightened. "What if he wore overalls over the one we have? That would hide the hem length. And a straw hat! Those are a dime-a-dozen at truck stops. I could cut slits in it and slip it right over the ears."

Katy laughed. "That would look cute."

"Do you think he'll do it?"

She shrugged. "Maybe." In actuality, she knew he would. Jasper didn't care if he embarrassed himself, so long as it was for a good cause. Making little kids smile was definitely a good cause. She just wasn't sure she wanted to ask him. It had been two days since they returned home, and they hadn't spoken since. He sent her a couple of "Thinking of You" texts, but it had been radio silence on their date. She didn't know what to make of it.

"Oh, I sense a story. What's that look?"

"Look? What look?" Katy turned away and reached for her plate.

"Don't be coy. You know what I'm talking about. Did something happen between you and that handsome ranch hand?"

Katy twirled pasta onto her fork as she formulated an answer.

"It did, didn't it?" Heidi squealed softly. "It's about damn time!"

"Grandma!" Katy chuckled.

"Don't 'Grandma' me. I've been waiting years for you to look at a man as something other than a friend or a colleague. You've been so focused on building a career you've forgotten to build a life."

Katy sat straighter. She'd never thought about her lack of relationships in that way before. But she could see what her grandma meant. She had a life, but she didn't.

"So, tell me about him. I remember his sister, but I didn't have him as a student. What's he like? I know he works for the Mitchells up at the Stone Creek, but what does he do in his free time?"

She twirled more pasta, a small frown on her face. "Um, well," she cleared her throat, "he's nice. I'm not too sure about the free time thing." She lifted the forkful of pasta to her mouth.

Heidi rolled a hand. "And?"

Katy's shoulders slumped. Her fork clinked against her plate as she dropped her hand holding the now empty utensil. "And a really good guy," she said with a sigh.

"Is that a bad thing?"

"For my mental stability, yes."

Heidi chuckled. "If you stop fighting your attraction, the effect will be good in the long run."

She shook her head and scooped up more of her dinner. "I don't know, Grandma. I mean, when am I supposed to find time for him? He asked me to go on a date—which I've already agreed to." She held up a hand to stave off Heidi's comments. "But I just don't know if it's wise to go through with it. He deserves a woman who can give him time and attention. It's eight-thirty and I'm just now eating dinner because I only got home thirty minutes ago. The man gets up with the sun every day, which means he probably goes to bed not far from now. How is an hour or so a night—on the nights we actually see each other—going to build a relationship?" She sighed again, a giant lump forming in her stomach. She put her plate on the table, suddenly not hungry anymore.

Heidi laid a hand on her back and rubbed small circles. "Sweetie, I know it seems daunting, but I think you owe it to both of you to try. If it's meant to be, you'll find a way to make it work. Don't throw away a chance at a life beyond work because of the what ifs."

A knock on the door cut off the conversation.

"Geez, I'm popular tonight. Hang on." She rose and went to answer the door. A quick peek through the peephole made her heart race. She stepped back, staring at the wood. What was he doing here?

Grasping the knob, she yanked the door open. "Jasper? What are you doing here?"

He smiled and held up a box of popcorn and a mason jar with a light brown powder in it. "I realized that our schedules are too busy, and yours is too unpredictable for us to really plan much, so I decided that impulsiveness was probably the way to go. You up for a movie date on your couch?"

Her eyes widened, traveling over his face to the items in his hands, then over her shoulder to where her Grandma stood by the couch, arms crossed and grinning.

"Oh."

She turned back to Jasper to see him looking past her.

"I'm sorry, Mrs. Beck. I didn't know you were here." He glanced at the driveway, then out at the street. "You didn't park in the drive, and I didn't give the car in front of the house any thought."

Katy looked past him, then at her grandma. "Why didn't you park in the driveway?"

"I didn't want to block your cruiser in."

Jasper looked at his truck. "I should probably move, then." He hesitated. "Though it looks like you're busy, so I'll just go."

"No, stay." Heidi waved a hand at him, then started putting things back into her box. "I just stopped to ask Katy a question. She answered it, so I'll be going." She hefted the box as she finished speaking and breezed past them. "You two have fun."

"Let me help you with that, Mrs. Beck." Jasper put the popcorn and jar down on the porch and followed her, reaching for the box.

"Oh. Well, thank you, Jasper."

Katy watched from the door as he loaded the box into the backseat of her grandma's car.

"Tell your sister I said hello." Heidi opened the driver's door.

"Yes, ma'am. I will."

"And you, young lady," she pointed at Katy, "don't forget my question."

Katy frowned, her eyes widening when Heidi pointed at Jasper. She'd been serious about the Easter Bunny suit? Oh, geez.

With a broad smile, Heidi waggled her fingers and got into the car. Jasper jogged back to the house and scooped up the popcorn and mason jar as she drove away.

"So." He shook the box of popcorn. "You, me, and a movie?"

The hopeful, boyish look on his face made Katy smile. She nodded and stepped back. "Sure."

Twenty-Two

The scent of a tomato-based sauce hit Jasper as he stepped inside. Rich and fragrant. "Did you just eat?"

"Yeah. I haven't been home long. Grandma stopped by not long after I sat down for dinner."

"Oh. Are you sure you're up for a movie? I can come back another night. I just came tonight because it's Saturday, and I was hoping you wouldn't have to work tomorrow morning." He frowned. "Do you? I guess I should have asked these things before I came inside."

She waved a hand and led him into the living room. "It's fine. I'll go in at some point tomorrow, but not right away. Not unless there's an emergency." She stopped and glanced at him, a rueful smile on her face. "Well, an emergency that requires my attention."

He chuckled.

"So, what's in the jar?" She picked up her dinner plate and headed for the kitchen.

"Hot chocolate mix. Sara makes it. James brought some over for Daisy and Asa one day, and Daisy made a thermos of it to send into the field with Asa. He shared, and I've been hooked on it ever since."

"I've had her hot chocolate at the diner. It's delicious. I'll heat up the water if you want to get a couple of mugs down." She pointed to a cabinet not far from him.

While she heated water in the teakettle, Jasper got out the mugs and put a bag of popcorn in the microwave. When the kettle whistled, she made two mugs of hot chocolate, then they carried their snack into the living room.

"So, what should we watch?" Katy sat down on one end of the couch.

Jasper sat down on the other end. He didn't want to crowd her, but he also didn't want to be too far away. This was supposed to be a date.

"You pick. My tastes run toward action films, but if you want to watch some sappy romantic thing, that's fine."

She arched an eyebrow, and one side of her mouth tipped up. "Do you promise not to fall asleep if we watch a movie like that?"

"They tend to be funny, so sure. A drama, though? Without any action? No guarantees."

"Noted," she chuckled, and picked up the remote, turning on a streaming service.

They flipped through the movies until they found a comedy that appealed to them both. Jasper watched it with half an ear, distracted by Katy's presence. Even though she looked exhausted again, her beauty shone through. Her smile lit up the room.

She glanced at him and caught him watching.

"What? Do I have hot chocolate on my shirt?" She frowned and looked down.

Jasper chuckled. "No." He leaned forward to tuck a stray lock of her hair behind her ear. He heard as well as felt the hitch in her breath as it puffed over his hand. "I just think you're beautiful."

A blush stole over her cheeks. "Thanks." Her eyes met his before her gaze darted away. She glanced at him again, then at the TV.

He let his hand fall, but shifted, bringing himself a little closer. "Tell me something?"

"What?"

"How does a woman who looks the way you do still blush when someone tells her she's beautiful? You should be so used to hearing it by now, it should hardly register."

Her blush deepened, but the set to her shoulders told him it was more from embarrassment than from pleasure.

"I'm sorry. Forget I said that."

"No." She laid a hand on his thigh. "It's okay."

The muscles jumped beneath her fingers, and he gritted his teeth, keeping his hands where they were. He wanted to hear what she had to say.

"I wasn't always what most people consider pretty. I was quiet in junior high and high school. And I was also taller than all the other girls, had braces and horrible acne. I also didn't get boobs until I was like fifteen." She glanced down at her chest. "They're still nothing special."

Jasper shifted again, trying to get himself under control as he thought about her figure. She was on the small side in terms of curves, but he thought she was perfect. Her athleticism showed in her sleek, toned body. It told him she worked hard to keep herself in shape, so she could be the best she could be at her job. "I like the way you look. I think I proved that in Salt Lake City."

Her pupils dilated as she met his heated gaze. She bit her lip and looked away. "Jasper."

He held up his hands. "I know. Slow. But slow doesn't mean I won't let you know how you make me feel. I don't want you to ever doubt that you do it for me. You should never wonder if I'm thinking about you when we're apart or that I find you wildly attractive."

Her breath hitched again. He laid a hand over hers and sat back, pointing at the TV. "You're missing the movie."

She blinked, then laughed. Shifting on the couch, she leaned into his arm, wrapping hers around it and laying her head on his shoulder.

He echoed her chuckle and relaxed into the cushions. "Popcorn?" He held up the bag.

In answer, she stuck her hand inside and took a handful.

They spent the rest of the movie chatting about the plot and characters, laughing at their antics. As it faded to the credits, Jasper didn't move. He didn't want to and lose the feeling of contentment that had settled over him as the movie played.

Katy yawned and snuggled deeper into his side. "Do we have to move?"

"No." He glanced over, meeting her gaze.

She stared up at him with her honey-colored eyes. They drifted to his mouth, then back up. Jasper's blood heated at the look on her face. He didn't dare move, though, and break the spell.

Staring at him a moment longer, she leaned forward, tipping her head up. She hesitated for only a moment before closing the distance and placing a soft kiss on his lips.

It poleaxed him just like the first time. He fought to keep his hands at his sides and not yank her to him and make it something more. She wanted to go slow. He'd do that or die trying.

She pulled away and looked at him through her lashes. "Thank you."

His forehead wrinkled. "For what?"

"For not pushing me. I just—I want to see if we can even

make a relationship work time-wise before we delve in too deep."

Oh, it was going to work. This woman had touched a part of his soul hidden deep inside and brought it to the light. She was never far from his mind now.

"Take the time you need. We'll figure it out." He turned his hand over in hers and squeezed, then released her and stood. He might be willing to take things slow, but that didn't mean his body agreed with his decision. It was time to go if he didn't want her to see just what she did to him.

She stood beside him. "You're leaving?"

"Yeah. It's late, and we both need to get some sleep."

Katy rolled her lips in, pressing them together, and nodded. "I'll walk you out." She turned and headed for the door. As she grasped the doorknob, she turned, raising a finger. "I almost forgot. Grandma wants to know if you'll be the Easter Bunny next Saturday for the church egg hunt."

His eyebrows shot up, and he pointed at his chest. "Me? Why?"

Katy shrugged. "The person who was supposed to do it backed out."

"And she asked for me specifically?"

"Well, we were talking about who could do it, then she not so subtly brought up our trip and asked if you'd be willing. I think she was trying to play matchmaker."

He grinned. "So, if I agree to this, are you going to tell her our relationship started because of her?"

She snickered. "That would be funny to let her think she's got all kinds of skill at manipulating me. But I already outed us. So, will you do it?"

"Will I fit in the costume?"

"No. But she has a plan to fix that. She wants you to wear overalls to hide the fact the bottom stops well above your ankles."

Jasper laughed, picturing the image in his head. "That would do it."

She let out a soft laugh. "So, will you?"

"Oh, sure. Why not? Just get me the details and I'll be there."

A bright smile lit her face. She opened the door. "I'll let her know. She'll be tickled to death."

"I'm just glad her plan was overalls. I heard about some of her costumes from Megan." He moved toward the open door.

"There have definitely been some epic ones."

He stopped in front of her. "I had a good time tonight."

Her smile turned sweet. "Me too."

God, she was beautiful. He leaned down the few inches that separated them and feathered a soft kiss on her cheek. He needed to touch her one last time before he left, but didn't want to snap the thread he had on his body's response to her. "I'll see you later?"

She nodded, stepping back. "Yeah. Goodnight."

He backed onto the porch. "Goodnight."

TWENTY-THREE

The smell of fresh coffee hit Jasper's nose as he stepped out of his bathroom. Wandering down the hall as he buttoned his flannel shirt over his gray tee, he headed for the kitchen. His sister stood in front of the stove.

"Hey, kiddo. What are you doing up so early?" He took a mug down from the cabinet and poured himself a cup of coffee.

Megan looked up from the frying pan. "I figured if I ever wanted to talk to you, I needed to get up at the butt crack of dawn."

He offered her a rueful smile. "Sorry. I've been busy."

"I noticed." She lifted the pan and dumped its contents onto a plate. "That's for you." She gave it a nudge toward him.

"Oh, thanks." He took the plate and grabbed a fork from the drawer. "Did you eat?"

She nodded. "I had some cereal. I wasn't feeling eggs this morning."

He sat down at the table on the far side of the room, then glanced at her, frowning at the defeated note in her voice. "You okay?"

Sighing, she sat down across from him, propping her chin in her hand. "Yeah. Sort of."

"What's wrong?"

Her nose wrinkled, and she picked at an imaginary spot on the tabletop with her thumbnail. "I'm just ready for it to be summer. I'm sick of school."

Jasper frowned. "You're sick of school? Megan, you love school."

"I used to," she mumbled.

"What changed?"

"Burke. He won't leave me alone."

Some of that fatherly instinct he'd cultivated over the years reared its head. "What's he doing, exactly?" She hadn't gone into detail with him yet about what was happening, and he'd been too preoccupied with work and his budding relationship with Katy to ask. Guilt soured his stomach. He vowed then to pay more attention.

She shrugged, still picking at the spot. "Calling all the time. Sending me little presents. He's showed up at the house too. But Izzy won't let him in and tells him I'm not home. We had to cover the garage windows so he couldn't look in and see my car."

Alarm bells went off in Jasper's head. He put his fork down. "Did you call the police to report the harassment?"

She snorted. "And say what? Officer, my ex-boyfriend keeps sending me stuffed animals and flowers to apologize for being an asshole cheater. He never threatens me."

"But he makes you uncomfortable."

"Doesn't matter. He's just annoying. Can't get a restraining order for annoying."

"Maybe you and Izzy should look into finding a new place to live. How much longer do you have on your lease?"

"Until July."

"What's the penalty for breaking it?"

"Um, a month's rent, maybe? And I think we forfeit our security deposit."

"If you want to move, I'll pay the penalty and give you the deposit for a new place." He'd do more than that if it meant keeping her safe. Burke might not be threatening her now, but if she continued to ignore him and blow him off, that could rapidly change.

Megan let out a soft growl and got up, going to the coffeepot. She picked up the carafe and refilled her mug. "I don't need you to do that. I think I'll be fine where I am."

"Megs—"

"I really just needed to vent to someone about it. Izzy hates his guts and just rants anytime he shows up. It's all super stressful, and I just needed to get away from it all—"

Jasper stood as she talked, walking over to her and enveloping her in a hug, effectively cutting off the words spilling from her mouth. She wrapped her arms around him and buried her face in his chest.

"I'm sorry." Her words were muffled by his shirt, but he heard the tears in them. He could also feel them soaking his shirt.

He rubbed her back. "It's okay, Megs. You don't have anything to be sorry for. I'm your big brother. You're supposed to be able to cry all over me when you need to."

She hiccupped and raised her head. A watery smile crossed her face. "Thanks, Jazz."

He squeezed her tight, then let go. She wiped the wetness from her cheeks and returned to the table with him.

"So, are you sure you don't want to find a new place? What about a new phone number?"

"I blocked his number, so those have stopped. Unless he borrows a friend's phone, anyway."

Jasper frowned again, not liking that the kid was going to such extreme measures to contact her.

She waved a hand as she saw his face. "I've stopped answering if it's a number I don't recognize. He just leaves a message, and I delete it without listening to it."

His frown didn't disappear, but he cut into his omelet. "Just be careful, okay? If he does anything weird, call the cops. And don't delete the messages. Get it on record, so you can show a pattern of escalation. That matters, okay?"

She nodded. "I will, I promise."

"Good. So, is he the only reason you needed a break from school?"

"Mostly. My classes suck. I can't wait until next year when I get to do more of the core classes for my major. Statistics is so boring."

"But it's important for a biology major." Megan was studying to become a vet. She'd always had an affinity for animals. Jasper knew she'd be great at it.

She sighed. "I know. Doesn't mean I have to like it, though."

He agreed with her there. He was good at math, but still didn't care for it.

The wrinkle between her eyebrows smoothed out. "So." She raised her coffee mug and gave him a playful smile over the rim. "I heard a rumor from Daisy you have your eye on a certain sheriff."

Jasper tilted his head, a half-smile on his face. "Maybe."

Megan's smile widened. "I think that's great. Daisy seems to like her, and she's pretty."

"She is, yes. She's very nice, too."

"I would hope so. So, when do I get to meet her?"

He shrugged and ate the last bite of his omelet. "We just started seeing each other. And she's pretty gun-shy about relationships."

"Why?"

"She doesn't think she has the time necessary to devote to

one. I wore her down, though, and convinced her to give us a try."

She chuckled. "Of course you did. Who could resist you when you turn on the charm?"

"Exactly." He laughed and rose to take his plate to the sink.

"You should invite her over for Easter dinner. Daisy would love it. You know she loves to cook for a crowd."

"I might. But she has her family to consider too. Which reminds me, Mrs. Beck says hello."

Megan smiled. "Mrs. Beck is my favorite teacher ever. Now I really want to meet Katy. I only know who she is because Mrs. Beck talked about her and had all kinds of family pictures on her desk."

"And you will. It just might not be until after you're out of school for the summer. We'll see, okay?"

Her mouth twisted, and she rolled her eyes. "Ugh. Fine."

He smiled. "I'm going to head to work. Thanks for breakfast."

She picked up a dishcloth and turned on the faucet. "You're welcome."

"I'll see you later." He headed for the mudroom to put on his boots and jacket, smiling. He might not like the reason she came home early for Easter break, but he was glad she was here.

Twenty-Four

Katy drove through the gates of the Stone Creek after Daisy buzzed her through. She headed for the main house to say hi to her before heading for Jasper's. She had his costume for Saturday.

Parking at the edge of the drive, she climbed out and headed for the front porch. Her boots thudded as she mounted the steps and crossed to the door. It opened as she raised her fist to knock.

Daisy smiled at her. "Hi, Sheriff. Come in, please."

"It's Katy, please." It felt weird having someone her own age address her by her title. Even when she arrested people her age, it felt strange. She was sure she'd get over it eventually, but she wasn't there yet. Besides, she hoped she and Daisy could become friends. Her brother James's fiancée, Sara Katsaros, was a mutual friend.

Daisy nodded as she stepped back. "So, what brings you out here. Looking for Jasper?" A knowing smile crept over her face.

Katy bit back a smile. Apparently, the grapevine was hard at work, speculating about their relationship.

"Yes, actually. My grandma asked him to be the Easter Bunny for our church's egg hunt this weekend. I have his costume. Plus, I wanted to say hello. It's been a few days since I've seen him."

Daisy gave her a curious look. "So, Sara mentioned Jasper asked her for a jar of hot chocolate a few days ago because he wanted to surprise you. She got the feeling you were dating. Are you?"

Katy let the grin loose. It was nice to know the grapevine didn't know *everything*. She held a hand out, tipping it back and forth. "Yes? It's very new."

"Oh!" She squealed. "That's fabulous. I don't know how I didn't know this. I mean, I kinda wondered, but he must not have told Asa, because he would have said something to me." She grabbed Katy's hands and towed her further into the house. "You need to tell me more about this. What's it like? Do you laugh a lot? Does he make your toes curl when he kisses you? *Has* he kissed you?"

Katy laughed at Daisy's rapid-fire questions.

They stopped at the kitchen island, and Daisy turned, giggling. "Sorry. My mouth runs ahead of my brain sometimes. But seriously, what's it like? He's a hunk. And funny."

"It's been nice. He's sweet. And yes, he makes me laugh. He's also not too bad of a kisser."

Daisy grinned, nudging the cookie jar toward Katy. "Have a cookie. They're chocolate chip."

Not about to turn down chocolate, she reached inside. "Thanks."

"That's great. Jasper's an awesome guy. I'm glad he's found you."

If she was honest with herself, Katy was glad too. She'd started thinking of things besides work in her off hours. When she was signing off on reports and filling out her own patrol logs while sitting on her couch before she went to bed, her mind inevitably strayed to him. She'd end up staring off into space, not working. It was usually at that point she fired off a text to him, just to say hello. Sometimes, he would call her and they would talk while she worked. They'd discuss their day or something they heard on the news. Light stuff that she could focus on while she typed up incident reports and reviewed memos and other things that came across her desk that she didn't have time to address at the office.

But she wanted to see him. The conversations only increased her desire to feel his arms around her and to see his smile.

"I'm glad things have worked out the way they have too. He's great." She took another bite of her cookie. "Do you know if he's home yet? I tried calling, but he didn't answer."

"They're still out somewhere. Asa said something about checking for calves. The season's just started, so their hours are getting longer as they keep a close eye on the herd."

"Oh." Disappointment settled in her belly.

"His sister's home, though, I think. You could wait for him. I don't think they'll be too much longer." She glanced at the clock. "Asa's usually in by seven, and it's almost that now."

Intrigue made Katy sit a little taller. She'd heard a lot about Jasper's sister, Megan, but had yet to meet her. "You know, that's not a bad idea." She straightened and popped the rest of her cookie into her mouth.

Daisy beamed.

"Thanks for the cookie."

"Anytime."

The two women walked back to the front door. Katy waved as she left, getting back into her cruiser to drive down the lane to Jasper's house. His truck was still missing—unless he parked in the garage—but a blue SUV sat in the driveway.

Getting out of her car, she made her way to the door and knocked.

The girl who answered had Jasper's dark hair, but her bright blue eyes were all her own.

"May I help you?" A curious frown lit her pretty face.

"Hi. I'm Katy Lattimer. Is your brother home?"

"Oh!" Surprise lit her face before she smiled. "I knew I recognized you. You're his new girlfriend. Come in." She stood back to let Katy enter, then closed the door.

"It's so nice to meet you. I'm Megan." She held out her hand.

Katy shook it. "You too. I've heard a lot about you."

Megan rolled her eyes. "I'm not sure that's a good thing."

Katy laughed. "It is. What he said was good. He's very proud of you."

Color tinged the girl's cheeks. "Good to know I haven't done anything too terrible." She motioned toward the living room. "Jazz isn't home yet, but let's go sit."

"Sure." Katy followed her in and sat on the couch. Megan perched on the large recliner and drew her legs up to tuck them under her hips.

"Tell me about yourself. I know next to nothing about you. He only mentioned you the other morning after I asked about you. Daisy mentioned she heard a rumor the two of you were dating, and I was curious, so I peppered him with questions."

Katy cocked her head. He hadn't mentioned her? She wondered why not. He'd been the one who was gung-ho to start a relationship. "Oh, well, what do you want to know?"

Megan shrugged. "Anything, really. Are you from here? I know Mrs. Beck is your grandma."

Katy smiled. "Yes, she is. And yes, I'm from Pine Ridge. Sort of, I guess. My parents met in high school. Dad joined the Army, and they moved around for a while. I was born in Germany, but we moved back here not long after. Dad owns the mechanic shop in town. My mom does his books and those for some of the other businesses in town. I have a brother too. Marcus. He's an Army Ranger stationed in North Carolina."

"How did you become a cop? And sheriff at such a young age? Or are you way older than you look?"

"I'm thirty-one. I was an MP—military police—in the Army for six years. After I was medically discharged, I enrolled in some criminal justice classes and went through the police academy. I've been with Boone County since then."

"Medically discharged?"

Katy nodded. "An IED took me out of the game." Her expression cooled. She still didn't want to talk about it. Megan noticed and moved on.

"Why did you decide to run for sheriff?"

"Actually, I didn't. Our previous sheriff died of a stroke. When the county commissioners looked into replacing him, they also discovered some shady stuff going on in the department when a former deputy came forward, claiming he'd been fired because he refused to trump up the charges on some local kids who kept joyriding through town. The sheriff wanted him to add marijuana charges to them. When he refused, the sheriff got someone to claim brutality and fired him."

"Whoa. I don't remember any of this. But I've been in Billings for two years. Did he ever try to get you to do anything like that?"

Katy shook her head. "I heard rumors about stuff he was doing, but no, he never did. I think he knew I wouldn't and because I was a bit of a local hero due to my military service, he left me alone. There were a few times I didn't agree with him, but he never asked me to cross a line."

"So, what happened after the deputy came forward?"

"The commissioners dug deeper and found that he'd been trumping up charges on a lot of people to inflate the crime rate in the county so he could get additional funding for the department. None of that funding went to hiring more deputies, though. It went toward gear purchases that he then sold under the table, pocketing the money."

Megan gasped. "And you had no idea?"

Katy shook her head. "Ray Hughes—my chief deputy—did, but he never said anything until after Lyons died. I don't think he wanted to lose his job. His entire family lives in Pine Ridge and so does his wife's. The only other ones who knew were two of the senior deputies. They helped him and received kickbacks in return. They've since been fired."

"Is that how you got the job?"

"Pretty much. Ray had seniority, but they were worried about his involvement in the situation, so they passed him over. My military record appealed to them, and so did my notoriety. I think the hope was my status as a war hero would help gloss over the corruption in the department. I took the job because I didn't want to see them bring in someone new who would try to snap the whip. I know the other deputies and have learned who I can trust. I've replaced a couple, and I have two, maybe three, slots to fill, but I wish I had a few more. The commissioners decided that the inflated numbers meant I didn't need a big budget and chopped it when they appointed me."

Megan wrinkled her nose.

"I finally convinced them with *my* numbers from the last couple months not to cut the few open positions I had. Now I just have to find time to interview candidates."

Megan shook her head. "I do not envy you."

Katy chuckled. "No one does."

The interior door from the garage opened. Katy heard two thuds as Jasper took off his boots. She turned, waiting for him to come through from the kitchen. When he appeared, her heart skipped as she took in the welcoming smile on his face.

"Hey. What are you doing here?"

"Phone calls weren't good enough for me anymore. Plus, I have your costume from Grandma."

"Costume?" Megan said. She looked between her brother and Katy. "What costume?"

Jasper groaned, coming around to sit next to Katy on the couch.

Katy laughed. "He's agreed to be the Easter Bunny for the church egg hunt on Saturday."

Megan's eyes widened. "Seriously?" A wide grin broke over her face. "Oh, this I have to see."

"It's in my car." Katy stood. "I'll be right back." She jogged out of the room before Jasper could protest. Megan wasn't the only one who wanted to see him in it. She wanted to take pictures too.

When she returned a minute later with the box, Jasper wasn't in the room.

"Where did he go?" She put the box on the couch.

"To put on some different clothes. Said he didn't want to get the costume dirty with his work clothes."

"Oh."

Megan got up to come over and look in the box. She lifted the outfit free. "Oh, this is fantastic."

Katy reached in and picked up the head. "Right?"

"I'm going to take so many pictures."

Katy laughed. "Me too."

Jasper returned, grimacing as he saw the white and pink outfit. "Oh, God. It's even worse than I imagined."

Katy laughed, her eyes roving over his broad chest and muscular legs highlighted by his tight blue t-shirt and gray athletic shorts. "It won't be that bad."

He gave her a dry look.

"It won't. Not until you put this on." She reached into the box and removed the straw cowboy hat her grandma found at a thrift store."

"Oh, man."

Grinning, Katy set the head down, then put the hat on top, drawing the ears through the slits Heidi cut in it. "There."

Megan laughed and pointed at her brother. "I love this. So much." She thrust the suit at him. "Put it on."

He grumbled, but took it. Unzipping it, he stepped in, working his feet through the holes. Pulling it up, he thrust an arm through, then the other, and zipped it. "Um…" He held out his arms. "Did she have a plan for this?" The sleeves stopped several inches above his wrists.

"It has mittens." She spun, digging in the box again to pull out a pair of long white mittens that looked like rabbit paws.

He took them from her and put them on. "They're a little snug, but they cover the short sleeves. I definitely need to wear overalls, though." He looked down at his feet. Four inches of hairy calf was exposed.

"Do you have some?"

He nodded.

"I know where they are." Megan spun on her heel. "I'll get them."

Katy smiled, watching her go, then looked at Jasper. She couldn't hold back the laugh.

"Laugh it up. I know I look ridiculous." A grin slashed his mouth.

"You do. But you also look cute."

A gleam entered his eyes. He stepped toward her, invading her space. "Cute, huh?"

She bit her lip and nodded. "Yeah."

Jasper dipped his head and kissed her. Explosions went off behind Katy's eyelids. She curled her hands into the soft fur covering his chest and held on.

"I suddenly have the urge to sing 'I Saw Mommy Kissing Santa Claus.'"

They jumped apart at the sound of Megan's voice.

"Except you're not my mom, and you're not Santa." She tilted her head. "Are there any songs about kissing the Easter Bunny?"

"Oh, can it, Megs." Jasper shook his head, a small smile tugging at one corner of his mouth. He took the overalls from her.

Katy smothered a laugh.

He sent a mock glare at her, then bent over to put on the overalls.

They made it just past his knees when he got stuck. "Dammit. I might need a bigger size to go over this costume."

"Just unfasten the buttons on the side." Megan pointed to them.

"It's not just the waist. I think they're going to be too snug in the thigh."

Katy stepped forward, reaching for the buttons. "Let's see if we can get these up first, and we can go from there." She helped him unfasten the buttons.

Once they were loose, he hopped, tugging on the fabric. It slid up, molding itself to his butt and thighs. She covered her mouth. *Oh my.*

"Yeah. I need a bigger size."

"Oh, I don't know Jazz. I hear sexy bunny is in." Katy's lips twitched as she tried to hold in her laughter. He really did look ridiculous.

The glare returned. Megan took his picture, and he turned it on her.

"Fasten the straps and put the head on, so we get the full effect." Megan reached in front of Katy and picked up the head, holding it out to him.

He sighed. "Really?"

Katy and Megan nodded.

Huffing, he buckled the straps, then took the head and put it on. "Happy?"

It was the muffled sound of his voice that sent Katy over the edge. She couldn't hold back the laughter anymore. Bending double, tears rolled down her face as she laughed. "I'm—I'm sorry," she gasped. "It's—the pants! And the hat!"

Megan laughed along with her and took more pictures. Jasper propped his mitten-covered hands on his hips, making them laugh harder. Katy dropped onto the couch. She brought her phone up and snapped a photo.

He took off the bunny head and put it under his arm. "Get it all out now. Can't have you laughing at the Easter Bunny on Saturday."

"Oh my God! My sides hurt!" Megan dropped into the chair. She wiped at her face.

Katy sat up, wiping at her own face. She looked up at him. A few more giggles escaped. "Are you—" She laughed again. "Are you going to be able to get those pants off?" They really were very snug.

A wicked smile lit his face. "Wanna help?"

Megan made a retching noise.

Katy just arched an eyebrow at him. "Sure. It's always been my dream to strip the pants off a hairy man."

His grin vanished as he gave her a disparaging look. "Funny. Help me take these off." He set the head down and unfastened the buckles, then hooked his thumbs in the sides and did a little shimmy.

Another burst of laughter pushed past Katy's lips. She waved a hand. "Sorry." Stifling another laugh, she reached for the fabric below his knees, where it was looser, and tugged. The pants barely budged. She sat back and glanced up. "Maybe you should unzip the suit and try to take it all off together. That might be easier."

He drew the zipper down and pulled his arms free. Megan grabbed the costume from behind while he pushed on the sides and Katy tugged in front. Between the three of them, they inched the fabric down past his butt, and it slid down his legs.

He stepped out of it with a huff. "I'm going to roast in that outfit."

"Maybe." Katy picked up the costume, pulling the suit free of the overalls. "It's supposed to be cooler this weekend. Sunny, but cooler."

"I hope so. I'll have to find a spot where I can take the head off and get some air, and the kids can't see me."

Megan patted his shoulder. "Well, now that I've had my laughs for the day, I'm going to head to my room and leave you two alone." She looked at Katy. "Thank you for embarrassing my brother. I think you and I are going to get along great."

Katy grinned. "I think so too."

Jasper sighed. "Great."

Megan laughed and waggled her fingers, exiting the room.

"I like your sister. She's fun."

"Only when she's not picking on you," he grumbled, then smiled. "But seriously, I'm glad you two hit it off." He turned and sank down beside her, putting an arm across the back of the couch. "So, are you able to stay for a while?"

Katy sat back and turned, putting a hand on his chest. "I think I could be persuaded to stay for a bit."

A hot gleam entered his eyes. "Yeah?" He leaned closer.

"Yeah."

TWENTY-FIVE

A shrieking child ran past Katy as she walked toward the picnic shelter at the park, carrying a bowl of pasta salad she made for the potluck. She smiled at the little girl, whose white-blonde hair flew out behind her as she ran from a boy she presumed was the girl's brother if his matching hair color was anything to go by. They were headed for the field where the egg hunt was about to start.

She found an empty spot on one of the tables and put the bowl down, then followed the kids. As she walked, she lifted her face to the warm sun. The air had a bite, but there was little wind. It was a glorious day for this.

Waiting for the Easter Bunny to signal with his flag that it was time to hunt eggs, the kids bounced, laughed, and talked at the top of their lungs. Nearing the mass of local children, Katy spotted Daisy and Asa standing off to the side, a tall blonde man and dark-haired woman with them. Daisy's aunt, Nori, and Asa's dad, Silas, were there too. Sparing a grin at Jasper in his getup—he looked fantastic and was hamming it up for the kids—she walked over to them.

"Hi, guys."

"Katy, hi." Daisy smiled and waved.

"I didn't know you would be here."

"We're here to cheer on Olive. Plus, it was too nice to stay home." Asa pointed to a dark-haired child squatted in front of the tall blonde man as she looked at the crocuses poking up through the grass. "That, and we had to see Jasper dressed as the Easter Bunny."

They all chuckled. The blonde man stepped forward, holding out a hand.

"Hi." He smiled. "I'm Knox Duvall. This is my wife Sofie and our daughter, Olive."

"Nice to meet you. Katy Lattimer." She shook his hand, then Sofie's.

"Sofie's my daughter," Nori said.

"Oh. Are you visiting?" She knew Daisy was from Chicago and only knew who Nori was because she married Silas.

Sofie shook her head. "Actually, we just bought a ranch here. Knox's old one had a fire—" She waved a hand. "It's complicated."

A soft frown wrinkled Katy's forehead, but she didn't press. "Okay. Well, welcome to Pine Ridge."

"Thanks." Sofie smiled.

A whistle blew, getting everyone's attention. She turned to see her grandma standing in the front of the crowd next to Jasper. She lifted a bullhorn.

"Okay, everyone. Who's ready to hunt eggs?"

A loud cheer went up.

"Wonderful! There are rules. Ten eggs each. Older kids—six and up—have to run to the back of the field before they can start collecting, so the little ones don't get run over." She looked at Jasper. "Are you ready, Mr. Bunny?"

Katy smothered a laugh as Jasper bounced and gave the green flag he held a little wiggle.

Asa couldn't hold back his laugh. "You took pictures, right?" She heard him ask Daisy.

"So many."

"Good."

Heidi raised her bullhorn again. "Okay. Let's have a fun egg hunt!" The kids cheered again as she ran off to the side.

Jasper raised his flag in the air. The kids watched, some of them yelling at him to drop the flag. He did a little wiggle, the tail on his costume bouncing through the hole he'd cut in the back of the overalls.

"Oh my God," Asa choked out. "He's never living this down."

Katy agreed. She took her phone from her pocket and turned it on video mode while he danced and bounced, working the kids up. They loved him. She had a feeling he was stuck playing the Easter Bunny every year now.

Suddenly, he paused, his arm high in the air holding the flag. The kids stilled, and he dropped his arm. They all took off at a run, the older ones sprinting past him. Olive ran onto the field not far from her parents and started gathering eggs into her basket. Peals of laughter and shrieks of delight filled the air as the children found eggs in the grass.

Katy excused herself from the others and went over to Jasper. He stood with her grandma, watching the kids, clapping his paws every once in a while.

"Hi, there, Mr. Easter Bunny. Nice tail."

His deep chuckle came from beneath the bunny head.

"You look like you're having fun."

"Yeah. But it's hot as hell in here."

She chuckled. "It'll be over soon."

"I still have to sit for more pictures."

Katy glanced at Heidi. "Grandma, do you think once the kids are done, you could announce the Easter Bunny needs a break?" He sounded like he could use a few minutes to drink some water and let the air hit his face.

"Sure. Why don't you go now? I'll make the announcement in a couple of minutes."

"Great. Thanks, Grandma." She tugged on Jasper's arm. "Come on. We can go out to my car and you can hide behind it so you don't disillusion any little kids."

He chuckled again, but followed her. She swung by the picnic shelter on her way to the parking lot to get him a bottle of water. They made their way into the sea of cars. She was glad she'd arrived last minute. At the back of the lot, there weren't many people.

Stopping next to her car, Jasper took off the bunny head. "Dear God, that feels good." Sweat plastered his dark hair to his head and left a sheen on his face. "I think I lost five pounds just in sweat."

She smiled and held out the water bottle. "Here."

"Thanks." He tugged off the mittens and put them in the head, then took the water. Twisting off the cap, he tipped the bottle up, gulping half of it down in seconds.

Katy's eyes went to his throat. Her own face heated as she watched the muscles move and his Adam's apple bob as he drank. Clearing her throat, she glanced away. "So, are you staying for lunch?"

He tipped his head down, only a quarter of the bottle left. "I was planning too, yeah, but I'm wringing wet under this suit. All the way down to my underwear."

Oh my. Katy rolled her lips in as she pictured that. Her cheeks grew hotter. "Didn't you bring other clothes? You can't be wearing jeans under there."

"No, I have shorts on. But my t-shirt is soaked, and I didn't bring an extra. Just an overshirt."

"So put the overshirt on without the tee."

"Where am I supposed to change?"

"Well, how were you going to change your pants?"

"I wasn't. I was just going to put my jeans on over the shorts."

"Oh. Well, you could get in the back of my SUV." She pointed at her car. "The windows are tinted, so it would be hard for anyone to see in." *Thank God.* She didn't think she could handle seeing Jasper in just his underwear. The swim trunks were bad enough.

He eyed the car as he finished his water, then shrugged. "Okay." He handed her the bottle. "I better get back to the party."

"Do you want me to put you together a plate of food, so all the good stuff isn't gone before you can change?"

"That would be great. Thanks."

She smiled. "You're welcome."

He took the mittens from the bunny head and lifted the head to put it on. Katy put a hand on it to stop him.

"Wait." She stepped closer, stretching up to give him a kiss.

"What was that for?" he asked when she pulled away.

A corner of her mouth tilted, and she shrugged one shoulder. "Just because." She laid a hand against his cheek. "You're a good man, Jasper Hendriks."

His quizzical frown smoothed out, and he smiled before leaning down to kiss her again. "Thanks. Hey, what do you say tomorrow after all our Easter celebrations are done, you and I watch another movie or play a board game or something? We can have a repeat of the other night at my house." He waggled his eyebrows.

Katy chuckled, even as heat flooded her face—and parts south. That night ended with a rather passionate goodbye kiss that left her insides quaking the entire ride back to Pine Ridge.

"Sure. So long as you wear the hat." She flicked the straw hat on the bunny head.

He laughed. "You got it." He put the head on, settling it over his shoulders, adjusting it so he could see. "Come on. Let's go immortalize me in every family's Easter pictures."

Giggling, she followed him back to the shelter house.

TWENTY-SIX

Shoulders drooped and her eyelids heavy, Katy turned onto her street. She wanted to climb into her oversize bathtub, relax her muscles, then go to bed and sleep for the next eight hours. The first two things would happen, but she highly doubted she'd get eight hours of sleep. Maybe six. It was already after eight. Her alarm went off at five. Maybe she could skip her workout in the morning. Just this once.

The twinge in her back told her that would be a bad idea. Her morning yoga and strength training kept her back and leg limber and cut down on the pain.

As she neared her house, a dark shape in front of her house chased away some of her sleep. She groaned as she recognized the dark blue pickup. She'd forgotten all about Jasper. He'd left her several messages, but she'd never listened to them or read his texts because she'd been so busy.

Backing into her drive, she cut the engine and got out. Locking the car, she eyed him as he rounded the hood of his truck and walked through the lawn toward her. "Hi. I'm sorry I never got back to you. This evening—it wasn't good."

A frown marred his handsome face. "You look like you're ready to drop."

"I am. I'm sorry. I think I need a rain check on our date."

He stopped in front of her and took her hand. "Come on."

"What are you doing?" He pulled her toward the house. "Jasper?"

"Trust me?" He glanced back at her.

"Of course. I just don't understand what's going on."

They walked up the porch steps, and he motioned to the door for her to let them in. She unlocked it and walked inside.

Dumping her keys and purse on the entryway table, she turned to him. "Jasper, I—"

He laid a finger over her lips. "I know you're not up for a date. And honestly, I didn't expect you to be when I called the station and heard you'd been out working a fatal accident."

She took his hand, pulling it away from her face to thread her fingers through hers. "Then why are you here?"

"To take care of you."

"Take care of me?" She gave him a quizzical frown.

He nodded. "I'm betting your back and leg are screaming at you. So, you're going to march that cute booty of yours to your bathroom and get into the tub. While you soak, I'll make you some dinner. Once you eat, you're going to let me rub down your back and leg before I tuck you into bed."

Her eyes widened with every word. She didn't know what to say. "Jazz—"

"No arguing, Katydid. Let me take care of you." He brushed a hand over the side of her face to bury it in her hair and cup the back of her head. "Please?"

It was the soft please that did her in. She was so tired. Not having to worry about what to eat—and ultimately settling on a peanut butter sandwich because she was so exhausted— sounded wonderful. She knew better food would help her recover from today's stressful events. That accident scene was horrific. A family of four died on the way home from their Easter celebration when they swerved to avoid a deer in the road. They not only hit the deer, they clipped a boulder and flipped several times.

"Fine." The starch left her shoulders.

"Good girl." He leaned down and pressed a kiss to her forehead. "Go get in the tub. I'm going to run out to my truck to bring in the groceries I brought." He shook a finger in her face. "Don't come out of that bathroom until I tell you to, got it?"

Some of her spunk returning at his dictatorial tone, she snapped her teeth at his finger, a smile tugging at her mouth. "So bossy."

He grinned. "You love it." Fire lit in his eyes, sending an answering flame through her body.

Hot damn. Schooling her features, she smiled back. "I plead the fifth."

With a laugh, he spun her around and gave her a gentle shove. "Tub. Now."

Katy sent him a saucy smile but kept moving. In her bathroom, she turned on the faucet to fill the tub, adding a squirt of her bubble bath, then went to gather her pajamas. Securing her gun in her nightstand, she walked to the dresser to get clothes, hesitating over what to wear. She thought about putting on some workout clothes or even a pair of jeans and a sweater, but scoffed at herself, then grabbed her shorts and one of the oversize t-shirts she normally slept in. He'd seen her in her pjs in Salt Lake. So what if it felt more intimate now? She was too tired to care.

After grabbing underwear and a sports bra—because she wasn't that brave—she went back into the bathroom and stripped out of her uniform. Piling her hair high on her head and securing it, she stepped into the hot water. Sinking beneath the bubbles, she leaned back, letting her head loll against the headrest as her body floated. "Oh, that's heavenly." She'd better be careful, or she could easily fall asleep.

Once the tub was full, she shut the water off with her toes. Sighing, she closed her eyes and let herself—mind and body—drift.

TWENTY-SEVEN

Jasper heard the water shut off. He glanced at the clock on the wall. Katy would get a good thirty-minute soak in while dinner cooked. When it had passed seven o'clock and he still hadn't received a reply to his texts or the voice message he left her, he'd called the station. The sergeant on duty told him she was at a fatal accident on the other side of the county.

As soon as he hung up, he'd raided his kitchen, knowing she probably skipped dinner. Even with the large lunch she likely had because of the holiday, he knew she'd be hungry. He didn't want her eating junk because it was easy after a day like today. So, he loaded a reusable grocery bag with stuff to make roasted salmon, a salad, and some wild rice, then drove to town to wait for her to get home.

The oven beeped. He glanced at it, then spritzed the salmon with lemon and dusted it with some Cajun seasoning. Topping it with some pats of butter, he slid the pan into the oven and set the timer. Next, he filled a small pot with water and set it on the stove to boil. While he waited, he measured out the rice and chopped lettuce for the salad. When the water boiled, he added the rice, then covered it. Done with dinner prep, he tidied up the kitchen.

"That smells good."

He glanced up. Katy stood in the doorway, looking sleepy but less weary. And cute in her oversize shirt and shorts. The urge to walk up and kiss her hit him, but he pushed it down. He wasn't here for that. She needed him to take care of her, not seduce her. "You're supposed to still be in the tub."

She gave him a soft smile and wandered in to sit at the island. "I was falling asleep, so I figured I better get out before I drowned. What did you make?"

The timer went off and he spun around, grabbing an oven mitt. "Salmon, rice, and a salad." He removed the sizzling pan and laid it on the stove.

"Yum. Thank you."

"You're welcome. What do you want to drink?" He took a spatula from the utensil jar next to the stove and slid it between the salmon skin and the flesh, then set the filet on a plate next to the salad.

"Water's fine. I'll get it."

He turned, pointing the spatula at her. "Sit."

She gave him a sassy look, but complied. "Bossy, bossy."

A grin covered his face. He turned off the rice and tipped it out onto the plate. "Here you go." He slid the plate in front of her and handed her a fork.

"Thanks. I'm starving."

"Did you eat the protein bar you carry around?" He arched a brow at her as he went to the cabinet to get a glass down for her water. He knew she carried one, having seen it when they were in Salt Lake City.

Forking up a piece of the fish, she gave him a sheepish look. "No."

"I don't know why you bother to carry it." He filled the glass from the fridge dispenser, then set it next to her plate.

"Sometimes I do. But usually only when I skip lunch, not dinner."

Jasper hummed. He sat down next to her.

"Aren't you going to eat?"

"I already did a couple of hours ago."

"Oh." She ate more of her salmon. "Well, thanks for cooking me dinner."

His eyes traveled over her face. "You don't look as exhausted. You're more relaxed."

"Yeah. The bath took care of the tension."

"You need to take better care of yourself." He reached out to twine a tendril of hair that escaped her bun around his finger.

A soft smile quirked her mouth. "Isn't that supposed to be my line? And aren't I supposed to be the one cooking for you after a long day?"

He returned her smile. "That's what all the movies tell us. But we're not like the movie couples. If we were, I'd be the cop."

"So, I'd be the ranch hand?"

He chuckled. "Not hardly. You'd be the ranch cook. Or maybe even an attorney. But not a cowgirl."

She harrumphed, then laughed. "I want to be the cowgirl. I look amazing in a cowboy hat."

"You can wear mine," he laughed.

"While you wear the bunny's straw hat?" She chuckled. "Where is it, anyway? You were supposed to wear it."

"I didn't have a good reason to ask your grandma to let me borrow it. I wasn't about to tell her it was to make me look sexy for her granddaughter."

Katy laughed. "Oh! That's too funny. She'd probably give you the whole suit, though, if she thought it would get me laid."

His eyes went wide, and Katy laughed harder.

"Don't look so shocked. She might be close to eighty, but she's no prude. She likes her bodice rippers."

Jasper felt his face grow hot. That was not something he wanted to think about. He shifted on his stool. "Talk about a libido killer."

She laughed again. "Sorry."

He gave her a wicked grin. "That's okay. You can make it up to me."

The forkful of rice paused on its way to her mouth. "What happened to dinner, then my rub down and tucking me into bed?"

"Well, you need a goodnight kiss." His smile grew as he watched a blush stain her cheeks and heat lick her eyes.

"Oh, you're dangerous. You'd fit right into one of those bodice rippers."

Jasper leaned forward. "One day, you're going to find out just how well."

She swallowed and her hand shook. A grain of rice fell off her fork to land on her plate.

He leaned back. "But not tonight. Finish your food."

At his grin, she gave him a dry look, the heat in her gaze banking. "You delight in torturing me, don't you?" She ate the rice, then scooped up more.

He snickered. "Very much so, yes."

Katy rolled her eyes. Jasper got up to get himself a glass of water. He needed to move and cool down. He wasn't kidding about the goodnight kiss, but he didn't want it to get out of hand, either.

When she was done, Jasper took her plate and put it in the dishwasher, along with the other dishes from earlier and those he'd found in her sink, then turned it on.

"Come on." He took her hands and tugged her off her stool. "It's time for bed."

She didn't resist as he held on to one of her hands and led

her down the hallway to her room. Nor when he crossed to her bed and pulled back the covers.

"In." He pointed at the bed.

She gave him another dry look, but complied, lying back against the pillows. "Happy?"

A smile slashed his face. "Nope. Flip."

"Huh?" A small frown marred her face.

"I said I'd rub your back and leg, remember?"

"Oh. Jazz, you don't have to. They feel better since I had my bath."

He just arched an eyebrow at her and stayed silent.

She huffed. "Fine." Rolling onto her stomach, she stuffed a pillow under her head and hugged it.

"Do you have some lotion around here?" He glanced around, but didn't see any.

"In the bathroom, on the sink."

He crossed to the bathroom and picked up the bottle from the counter. Flipping open the lid, he sniffed it. More peaches.

A soft groan escaped him. Maybe this wasn't such a good idea.

But a promise was a promise. Even though he hadn't really promised. Sighing, he eyed her prone form, debating the best way to do this. Lifting a knee, he eased down next to her, tucking his leg under his body to sit. He squirted some of the lotion in his hand and decided to start with her leg. It seemed like the safest spot.

Warming the lotion in his palms, he covered her calf with his hands. The smooth skin was broken by thin scars and bumps of scar tissue. He could feel the knots as he worked his hands over the muscle. She moaned as he pressed in with his thumbs, running them the length of her calf.

"Did I hurt you?" He paused.

"No. It feels good."

Jasper continued his ministrations until the knots were

gone and only the hard scar tissue remained. Shifting, he eyed her back. He was in the wrong position to rub it effectively. He rose to his knees and straddled the backs of her thighs.

"What are you doing?" She lifted her head to look at him.

"Rubbing your back." He lifted the hem of her shirt. More scars crisscrossed her back. Some of them were small and puckered, while others were long and thin. His heart ached for what she'd been through, and admiration filled him for the strength and resiliency she showed. The woman seriously amazed him. Every day.

He added more lotion to his hands, warming it up, then pressed his palms to her back. The muscles jumped beneath his hands, but she quickly relaxed as he moved them over her skin, digging his fingers into the tight bands of muscle. Once he had her lower back relaxed, he moved higher, sliding his hands under her sports bra to get to her shoulder blades. The stretchy fabric slipped up, bunching under her arms. She moaned again. The note of pleasure in her tone quickened his heartbeat and sent his blood pumping south. He clenched his teeth against the spreading fire. This wasn't about him.

Too busy concentrating on keeping his body in check, he wasn't prepared for her abrupt roll. One second, he was massaging her back, the next, his hands cupped her bare breasts.

He sucked in a breath and bit back a groan. "Katy."

Her hands tangled in his shirt front and pulled him down. Inches from his mouth, she paused. "I want my goodnight kiss now."

Dear Lord, he was a goner. He nodded once and kissed her, thrusting his tongue past her parted lips to taste her heat. She kissed him back as aggressively as she'd demanded the kiss. Jasper wasn't complaining. He squeezed her breasts, rubbing his palms over the taut peaks.

She moaned and rocked her hips. He throbbed behind his zipper.

He broke their kiss to stare down at her. "Damn, woman." Her amber eyes glittered in the overhead light. He swallowed, throwing a rein on his desire. They needed to stop before this got out of hand.

"Yeah," she breathed.

He placed a tender kiss on her lips, trying to bank some of the heat, then removed his hands from under her shirt, tugging her bra back into place. "I should go." Climbing off of her, he stood beside the bed and adjusted himself. Katy's eyes went dark, and he bit back a moan. Definitely time to go.

Picking up the edge of the blanket, he flipped the covers over her, then leaned down, putting a fist on either side of her torso. "Get some rest."

"I will." She reached a hand up to touch his face, trailing her fingers over his lips. "Thank you for dinner. It was delicious. And much better than the PB and J I was planning to fix."

Satisfaction warmed him, glad that he'd made her evening better and taken care of his woman. He smiled against her fingers.

The last words of his thought rang through his head. *His woman.* That's what she was. He didn't know when it happened, but he'd laid claim to her. She was entrenched in his heart and was rapidly digging toward his soul.

He took her hand in his and kissed her fingers, then tucked it under the blanket. "Goodnight, Katydid."

She smiled softly. "Goodnight, Jasper."

Leaning down, he pressed a kiss to her forehead, then straightened. "I'll call you tomorrow. We'll make plans for a real, honest-to-goodness date, okay?"

"That sounds nice."

Trailing a finger down her cheek, he tapped her nose. "Get

some sleep." He stepped away from the bed, turning to leave the room. At the door, he glanced back. She watched him. "Goodnight."

Her fingers waved from around the top of the covers. "Night."

He shut off the light and left the room, closing the door behind him. In the hallway, he paused, blowing out a breath. A smile lit his face. He was in deep and loving every second.

TWENTY-EIGHT

"Axe throwing?" Katy peered up at the sign on the building they stood in front of. "We're going axe throwing?" They were in Billings and had just eaten at a great little pub. When they finished, he told her the date wasn't over yet, and drove them here. "Don't you get enough of physical labor on the job?"

He grinned and held the door open for her. "I throw around feed sacks and hay bales, not axes. Come on." He motioned to the open door with a quick flick of his head.

Katy gave him a skeptical look as she preceded him inside, but secretly, she was delighted. She'd never thrown axes, but she'd thrown knives while on active duty. It helped pass the time.

She glanced around as they walked up to the reception desk. Wood walls and chain-link fencing filled the room beyond the desk, creating lanes where groups stood, throwing tomahawk-style axes at targets painted on the wood walls. Laughter, conversation, and music flowed through the space, accompanied by the hard thwack of the axes hitting the wood.

"Hi." Jasper smiled at the clerk. "Reservation for Hendriks."

"For two?" the girl said, clicking through a couple of screens on the terminal.

He nodded.

"Okay. Follow me." She led them deeper into the building to lane four, where another employee waited on them.

"This is Milo. He'll be your coach. Have fun."

They thanked her, and she left.

The young man smiled at them. "Hello. As Carrie said, I'm Milo."

"Jasper." He held up a hand. "This is Katy." He motioned to her, and she waved.

"Nice to meet you both. Let's get started. Do either of you have any axe-throwing experience?"

"Does goofing around in the pasture with a wood axe count?" Jasper's mouth quirked.

Milo smiled. "Kind of. But we're using a much smaller axe." He looked at Katy. "How about you?"

"No. Just knives."

"When have you thrown knives?" Jasper looked at her.

"It was how we passed the time when I was deployed. Cards got boring after a while."

"This is a little different than that," Milo said. "The motion is more in the arm than the wrist. Why don't you each grab an axe, and we'll take some practice throws before we play some games?"

They did as he suggested, and Katy soon found herself having a great time. The kid had a wicked sense of humor, and the games were fun.

She glanced at Jasper. He didn't seem to be having as much fun as she was, though. Not because he didn't enjoy the activity, but because she had a feeling something was bothering him. She just didn't know what. All through dinner, he'd been quieter than normal. At first, she thought he was just tired, but the pensive look on his face told her otherwise. She'd hoped he would tell her what was wrong, but so far, he'd been mum.

They finished their session—each winning one game apiece—and left the venue. Now that they weren't laughing and competing, his frown returned deeper than before.

Katy settled into her seat in the truck, staring out the window as he drove from the city. Once they were away from the traffic, she turned in her seat.

"So, do you want to tell me what's bothering you?"

He glanced at her in the darkened interior of the truck. "What do you mean?"

"I mean, there's been a tiny frown between your eyes most of the night. What's wrong?"

He sighed. "I'm sorry. I was trying to put it out of my mind, so I didn't put a damper on our evening."

"It's okay. Just tell me what's bothering you."

"Megan."

"Your sister? Why? Is she okay?"

"She's fine. Sort of. Remember how I told you she broke up with her boyfriend?"

Katy nodded. "He's still bothering her?"

"Yeah. He's been leaving messages—from friends' phones because she blocked his number—sending her gifts, waiting for her when she gets out of class, that sort of thing. Even after she came home early for break to give them some space. She called earlier today just to vent her frustrations with it all."

Katy frowned, not liking the sound of that. "Has she called the police to report the harassment?"

He nodded. "I made her last week. There's not much they can do, though. He hasn't threatened or harmed her. Just annoyed her."

"If the pattern of harassment is strong enough, she might

be able to get a restraining order. In the meantime, tell her to walk with a friend, especially at night. And not to answer the door."

"I already did. I'm just glad she'll be out for the summer in a few weeks. She was going to stay in Billings, but she's not now. I guess she talked to Sara already and is going to work at the diner."

She laid a hand on his arm. "I'm sorry. I know this must be hard for you."

"Yeah. I know she can handle herself, and she knows to be cautious, but there's still a part of me that wants to turn the truck around and go find that kid, so I can beat the ever-living snot out of him." His hand clenched the steering wheel and a muscle in his jaw ticked.

Katy gave his forearm a squeeze. He took his hand off the wheel to thread his fingers through hers.

"I'm sorry for being moody."

"You really weren't that bad. I just noticed because you so rarely seem perturbed by anything. Stuff kinda rolls off of you, I've noticed."

The right side of his mouth lifted. "Normally, it does. But when it comes to Megan?" He shook his head. "That's a little harder to shake."

"She's lucky, you know. To have a brother like you. Things could have been so different for her if you hadn't been around, or if you hadn't stepped up and taken her in."

"I know, which is why I did it. Foster parents wouldn't have loved her nearly as much as me."

Emotion made Katy's heart swell as she listened to the conviction in his voice. Jasper loved deeply, she'd discovered. There wasn't anything he wouldn't do for someone he loved.

She couldn't help but wonder where she stood on that scale. Or if she would ever reach the same level as his sister. One thing was certain, he was nearing the top of hers. He was such a good man. Kind, generous, attentive. He made her feel important. From the start of their relationship, she'd never felt like an outsider in his life. He'd embraced her presence and folded her into his days like she'd always been there.

It had taken her longer to get there with him, but now, she carved out time for him each day. Even if it was just a phone call before she went to bed and some texts throughout the day. She cared, and she hoped he knew that.

Settling into her seat, she kept hold of his hand. His shoulders were still a bit rigid, but the furrow between his eyes had eased some now that he'd unburdened his worries to her. Contentment washed over her as a sense of rightness built deep within her. This was where she belonged. With this man. And he with her.

TWENTY-NINE

Voices echoed through the barn as the hands settled their horses into their stalls for the night. Jasper hurried through his routine, eager to get home so he could shower and change. He had plans with Katy.

The past few weeks had been wonderful with her. They spent time together whenever they could, even going out of their way to surprise the other with dinner or lunch. And they made it a point to plan a real date once a week. Sometimes it was last minute and not much more than dinner at Sara's or at the restaurant at the ski lodge, but they ditched their work clothes for something nicer and enjoyed each other's company away from their houses.

Tonight, he planned to take her stargazing. His sister had a friend affiliated with the local astronomy club in Billings. She'd set the whole thing up for him.

He finished dressing down his horse, then made sure he had hay and water before leaving the barn, doing his damnedest not to run across the yard and down the lane to his house. The last thing he needed was one of the other hands—

or Asa—wondering why he was running down the road in his boots and not his running shoes.

Letting himself into the house, he headed straight for the bathroom to take a shower, whistling as he went.

~

The radio in Katy's cruiser crackled to life as she turned off of County Road 12 onto the main highway into town.

"Sheriff, what's your location? Over."

Katy picked up the mic and radioed her location.

"Copy. Can you swing over to the O'Toole residence? Misty called and said Johnny's drunk and on a rampage again. Over."

"Oh, for the love of—" she muttered to herself. She'd been so close to being off-shift. "Dammit." She lifted the mic. "Yeah. I'm on my way. Send me another unit. I'll probably need it. Over." Johnny O'Toole was notoriously difficult to deal with when he was drunk. He'd get a bee in his bonnet and it would take three officers to subdue him. She just hoped that this time he hadn't laid a hand on Misty or their kids.

"Copy. I'll get backup en route. Over."

"Thanks. Lattimer, out." She set the mic back in its cradled and did a U-turn. The O'Tooles lived up the mountain, down a two-track dirt road. She was only five minutes away.

As she drove, she punched the button on her steering wheel that connected her phone to the car. "Call Jasper." She was going to be late for their date.

His phone rolled to voicemail, so she left a quick message explaining the situation and said she'd call him when she was free. Hanging up, she made the turn onto the O'Tooles' road, slowing as she neared their property. Three of their kids were in the front yard, huddled behind a tree.

That's unusual.

She'd never seen them do that before, and she'd responded to this house several times.

She slowed more, parking off to the side so she wasn't directly in line with the door, and got out. One of the kids—the middle one, she thought—peeked out from behind the tree, tears on his face.

"Daddy has a gun. He threatened to shoot Mama."

Curses flew through Katy's head, and her hand went to the butt of her weapon. "Where are your older brothers?"

"In the house. Mikey tried to step in front of Mama, and Daddy hit him. He's passed out on the floor. We ran out, but Noah was on the wrong side of Daddy to get out with us. He's in the corner with Mama."

Concern tightened her muscles. She nodded. "Okay. Take your sisters and go get behind my car. Stay behind the front wheels, okay?" She wanted as much metal between them and their father as possible if Johnny started shooting.

The boy nodded and herded his sisters away from the tree. Katy took her radio off her shoulder and called dispatch to advise them of the situation, and to have them tell her backup to step on it.

She lifted her gun free of its holster and jogged toward the house. She wasn't going in yet, but she'd like to get a lay of the land inside if she could.

Staying low, she peered over the windowsill into the living room. Johnny stood with his back to her, pacing as he muttered to himself. Empty beer cans littered the floor. She could just see the bottom of Misty's legs. She sat on the floor with her knees drawn up, one of her feet tapping the wood beneath. There was no sign of the boys.

Suddenly, Johnny whirled and pointed his weapon at Misty.

"No, no. Don't do that," Katy muttered. Dammit. She wanted to wait for backup.

A hand flopped near Misty's feet, and Katy realized she was cradling her unconscious son.

"Just shut up, bitch!" Johnny's voice carried through the closed window. "He'll be fine. Stop your whining." He raised the gun again. "Or I'll stop it."

Misty's reply was muffled. Johnny's hand clenched around the gun, and he rocked back and forth on his heels before he kicked his wife's feet and shouted at her again to shut up. Katy didn't wait to see what else he would do. She moved to the front door and tried the knob. It turned easily in her hand.

Pushing the door open, she stepped inside, gun trained to her left, into the living room.

"Johnny." She stepped into the open, drawing his attention. "Put the gun down, Johnny. Let's take a walk outside, and I'll get some help for your son, okay?"

He spun around. Katy's heartbeat quickened as he leveled the gun at her.

"Well, if it ain't the purdy new sheriff lady. Why are you here?"

"Because we heard you were drinking again and acting a fool. Why don't you put the gun down so we can talk?"

"I can talk with the gun."

"Okay, fine. Let's talk. Why are you upset?"

"Because my wife's a dumb bitch, that's why." He turned sideways, swinging the gun back to point at Misty and the boys. She had Michael half in her lap. Blood trickled from a wound at his temple. Noah huddled against his mother, brown eyes pleading with Katy to help them.

"That's not very nice, Johnny. What happened to upset you?"

He turned back to her. "All I wanted was to watch the game on TV in peace and have a few beers. She told me I'd had enough because I drank all we had. I told her to go get more, but she made up some excuse for why she couldn't leave."

"It wasn't an excuse, you bastard. Your dinner would have burned if I left."

Johnny turned, the gun wavering in his hand as he swayed on his feet. Katy's heart leaped into her throat, sure he was going to accidentally pull the trigger in his drunken state. He steadied his aim, though, and glared at Misty. "Shut your damn mouth, Misty. I didn't ask for your opinion."

"It's not an opinion. It's the truth," Misty shot back.

"That does seem reasonable, Johnny," Katy said. She wanted his attention on her. She was the one wearing a vest.

Johnny spun her way. He hiccupped, frowning. "Maybe so. But she should have bought more at the store today. She knew I was gonna watch the ballgame tonight. And these fucking rug rats wouldn't be quiet, either." He motioned to his sons, frowning harder as he realized three of the kids were missing. "They kept arguing over who got the next turn on the PlayStation. So, I got my gun out and shot it. Now, no one gets a turn. And they shut up." He shook his head. "You'd think a woman with five kids would be a better parent and know how to make her kids behave. Guess that's why it's up to the dad to do the disciplining. They listen to me."

"Because they're afraid of you, dumbass," Misty muttered.

Red colored Johnny's cheeks, and he swung toward his wife. "What did you say?"

Katy clenched her teeth. Misty was not helping. "Johnny! Ignore her. Look at me. You're talking to me, remember? Telling me why you're upset?"

"You know what?" He turned the gun on her. "I'm done talking to you. Get out of my house."

"I can't do that, Johnny. You know I can't."

Fear skated down Katy's spine as his eyes suddenly went clear and the slight shake in his hand disappeared.

"Fine." He pulled the trigger.

Pain blasted through Katy's chest. She fell backward, slamming into the wall. Her gun dropped from her hand and skittered several feet away. Unable to breathe, she slid to the floor, grimacing. Misty and Noah's screams echoed around her as Johnny turned on them.

Katy's breath came back with a gasp. Fire shot through her ribcage with the movement. She winced and rolled onto her knees. Oh, she had not missed this feeling.

Sirens split the air. She looked up at Johnny. He stiffened as he heard them too, then turned rage-filled eyes on her, lifting the gun once more. But this time, he pointed it at her head. Katy didn't wait to see what he would do. She pushed off the wall with her feet and tackled him, wrapping her arms around his waist. He fell back, and the gun discharged. Plaster from the ceiling rained down on them. Misty and Noah screamed again.

Katy ignored it all. She climbed up Johnny's frame, the pain in her chest fading to a dull roar as her adrenaline spiked. Wrapping her hand around his wrist, she slammed his hand into the floor and straddled him. The gun went off again, the bullet slamming into the wall. He bucked beneath her, but she kept her grip on his arm, using her other hand to block the punches he tried to throw at her.

Locking his hand under her arm, she bashed his other hand against the floor once more, harder than before. The gun fell from his grip.

He didn't stop fighting, though. His now free hand shot up as he took another swing at her. Katy leaned back at the last second, and his fist glanced off her chin. Still holding his left arm, she drew her taser and pressed it to his chest.

"Stop fighting me or I'm going to tase you."

He called her a bitch and bucked, trying to throw her off. She pulled the trigger. His body convulsed beneath her, then went limp as she let off the trigger. While he was stunned, she rolled him, bringing his left arm with her. She reached for her cuffs and got one bracelet secured around his wrist before the starch came back to his muscles. He started fighting her again, so she pulled the trigger on the taser once more. Convulsing, he grunted, then moaned when she let up.

"Stop fighting." Manhandling his other arm out from under him, she slapped the handcuff on it and sat back.

Wincing, she got to her feet. Her radio had come free from her shoulder in the scuffle. She grabbed the cord and hauled it back up over her shoulder.

"Dispatch, this is Sheriff Lattimer. Send medical to my location for a taser deployment and a head wound. Also advise them I took a shot to the vest. Over." She probed her chest, feeling the ridge where the bullet embedded itself in her Kevlar. It was hot too.

"Dispatching medical. Sheriff, are you okay? Over."

Katy held her side as she tried to catch her breath. "I'm fine. Just get them here. Lattimer out." She hooked the clip to the strap on her shoulder and pulled out her handcuff key to lock Johnny's handcuffs. Glancing up, she caught Misty's gaze. "Are you guys okay?"

Misty's eyes watered. "Mikey still won't wake up."

The sirens that had been growing steadily closer screamed up the driveway. Katy brushed her bangs back from her forehead and blew out a shaky breath as her adrenaline ebbed. "Help is here. We'll get him taken care of."

Through the front window, she could see her deputy come to a halt outside. Boots pounded up the wooden porch steps, and Ray appeared.

His astute gaze darted around the room before settling on her. "You okay, Lattimer?"

"I'm fine. Can you put him in your cruiser? I want to take a look at Mikey. And get a hold of the ambulance crew. Find out how far away they are." She ejected the prong pack from her taser and tucked it into Johnny's back pocket. The medics could remove the prongs from him.

Ray nodded and stepped closer, bending to grab Johnny's arm and help him stand. "Come on, O'Toole."

Johnny got to his feet, face red and rage burning in his eyes. "I'll get you for this, Sheriff. People will see what a mistake it was to appoint a woman sheriff. You're weak! All women are weak." He looked at his wife. "Especially you, bitch! You called the cops. Don't think I'll forget." Spittle flew from his lips as he tossed threats at Misty. He tried to turn out of Ray's grip, but the deputy was having none of it. In one swift movement, he slid his hand off Johnny's bicep and under his arm to put a hand on the back of his head. With his wrists cuffed, it forced Johnny to bend to take the pressure off his shoulders.

"That's enough, O'Toole. You're just digging yourself a deeper hole. Come on." He gave a tug against Johnny's arm and marched him out the door.

Katy picked up Johnny's gun, ejecting the mag from the weapon and securing both in one of the pockets of her pants. She'd log it into evidence after she checked on Mikey. Moving toward Misty and her sons, she knelt next to them and took Mikey from Misty's arms, laying him on his back on the floor. "How long has he been out?"

"Probably twenty minutes. When Johnny got the gun, I called for help."

"What did he hit him with?" She took her penlight from the pocket on her uniform shirt and lifted Mikey's eyelids, checking his pupillary response. It was sluggish, but even.

"The butt of the gun."

"Is he gonna be okay, Sheriff?" Noah's soft voice interrupted her evaluation.

She looked up at the boy and smiled. "He should be fine. I

think he has a concussion. We'll get him to the hospital, though, and have the doctors there check him out. Make sure that's all it is, okay?"

The boy sniffed and nodded.

"What about you? Are you hurt?"

"No, ma'am."

"Okay. Your other siblings are outside behind my cruiser. Why don't you go out there and let them know what's going on? I'm sure they saw Deputy Hughes take your dad out to the car in handcuffs, but I bet they'd like to hear it from you that everything is okay now."

Noah nodded. "Yeah. Okay." He got to his feet, then left the house after a long look at his mom and brother.

"Misty, what do you want me to do with the kids? You should probably accompany Mikey to the hospital. Do you want to take them all with you?"

The other woman's mouth flattened into a thin line as she fought back tears. "I'll call my mom. They can go with her."

"All right. How about you do that now and get her on her way over? I can wait with them here if she's coming right away. Otherwise, they'll need to come back to the station."

Misty nodded and started to rise.

Katy laid a hand on her arm. "Will you let me put you in contact with a domestic abuse counselor, who can help you? Johnny's not coming back anytime soon, since he shot me. You're going to need assistance without his income. They can help you separate your life from Johnny's too. Divorce, new house, all of that. If that's what you want."

A tear leaked from the corner of Misty's eye. "I don't know how I'll support all of us," she whispered.

"They'll help you figure that out. That's what they do. They have job placement services and education programs, if you need them, to help you get a decent job."

Misty blew out a breath through pursed lips. "I'm scared."

"I know. But you need to step up for your kids. They deserve that." She motioned to Mikey, who laid between them, still unconscious.

More tears spilled from the woman's eyes. "He was so brave. Trying to save me." She closed her eyes for a brief moment. "He's always been my protector, but Johnny's never hit him before."

"Maybe he sees him as a threat now. He's fourteen. He's not a little kid anymore." Mikey O'Toole was nearly six feet tall. Still gangly, the boy had a wiry strength. Katy doubted he could take on his dad in a fight yet, but it wouldn't be long.

"No." Misty brushed at Mikey's dark hair. "He's not." She drew in a shaky breath, then looked at Katy. "Okay. Put me in contact with whoever you want. I can't let this happen to my kids again. I never should have in the first place. I just didn't know how I'd make it on my own. I still don't, but now I don't really have a choice. And you're right. I need to put Johnny and my marriage in my past so my kids have a better future." Offering Katy a small, sad smile, she got up to find her phone and call her mom.

Katy blew out a breath of relief, both at the fact she was alive, and at Misty's capitulation. Hopefully Misty and her children would thrive now that Johnny would be locked up for a long time.

Mikey stirred, drawing her attention. He moaned, and his eyelids fluttered.

"Mikey?" She patted his cheek. "Hey. Can you open your eyes? It's Sheriff Lattimer."

The boy blinked, squinting up at her.

"Do you know where you are?"

He stared at her, confusion all over his face as he processed her words, before he glanced around and tried to sit up.

She pressed a hand to his shoulder. "Stay down. You've got a head injury. Your dad hit you. Do you remember?"

He raised a hand to his temple. "Not really."

"Do you know where you are?"

"Home."

"How about what day it is?"

"Um, Thursday?"

It was Saturday. Katy smiled and moved on to another question. "How about what month it is? Can you tell me that?"

"August." He frowned. "No. That's not right." He closed his eyes, covering them with a hand. "My head hurts."

"I know, honey. There's an ambulance on the way, okay?"

"Where's my mom?"

"She went to call your grandma to stay with your siblings, so she can go with you to the hospital."

"What about my dad?"

"He's in the back of a patrol car."

"Good." His voice was hard. Katy didn't blame him. She patted his knee.

Two ambulances arrived not long after her second deputy. The first crew packaged Mikey up and headed for the hospital. Katy corralled the rest of the O'Toole children in the kitchen and gave them snacks while the second crew took care of their father's taser injuries.

"Sheriff?"

She glanced up. A male EMT stood in the kitchen doorway.

"We're ready to take a look at your injuries, ma'am."

"Okay. Give me a couple minutes. I'll meet you outside."

He nodded and left. Katy turned to Noah.

"Are you okay alone in here with your siblings for a bit?" The twelve-year-old had done a remarkable job composing himself after she sent him outside, but he was still just a kid.

The boy nodded. "Yeah. We're just going to stay right here."

"Okay. If you need something, come find me or one of my deputies."

"I will."

She gave the boy a smile, then left the kitchen, walking down the hall and out the front door to her car. She needed to log Johnny's gun into evidence, then she'd let the EMTs look at her.

Opening the trunk, she took out an evidence bag and put the gun and magazine inside. Ray jogged over as she wrote on the bag.

"Hey. I'm heading back into town with O'Toole. Are you sure you're all right?" Concern shone from his dark blue eyes.

"I'm sure. I'll have a wicked bruise and be sore for a while, but that's it. I don't even think the bullet broke any ribs. I can already move better."

"Okay. Do what they say, huh?" He pointed at the ambulance.

A corner of her mouth kicked up. "I'll try." She held out the evidence bag containing the weapon. "Could you log this into the evidence lockup for me?"

"Yep." He took it, using her pen to sign his name to the chain of custody on the bag.

"Thanks. I'll see you at the station."

He handed her back the pen, then gave her a quick two-finger salute and turned around. Katy closed the trunk, then walked across the yard to the ambulance. She opened the door and climbed inside.

The EMT patted the stretcher. "Have a seat, Sheriff."

She perched on the sheet-covered gurney, extending her legs in front of her.

"My name is Chris. Can you remove your uniform shirt and vest?"

Katy unbuttoned her shirt, pulling it free of her pants, then shrugged it off her shoulders. The velcro of her vest made a loud rasp as she pulled the straps free. Slipping it over her head, she set it on the bench beside the gurney, leaving her in just her black undershirt.

Chris wrapped a blood pressure cuff around her arm and pumped it up. It was probably high. So was her heart rate. Adrenaline was a bitch.

The cuff hissed as he let the air out. "It's on the high end of normal, but considering what happened, I think you're good. Let's get the rest of your vitals, then I'll check out your ribcage." He took her pulse, counted her respirations, and ran a thermometer over her head, charting them all on the sheet of paper attached to a clipboard. Other than her pulse, every-thing was fine.

"Okay. Where did the bullet hit?"

Katy pointed to the upper swell of her left breast. Johnny's aim had been dead on. If she hadn't been wearing a vest, this conversation wouldn't be happening.

Chris let out a low whistle. "Okay. Do you know what caliber?"

"It was a twenty-two." For which she was grateful. It's probably what saved her from broken ribs.

"Lift up your shirt for me."

She pulled her left arm free of her t-shirt and raised the hem to her neck, exposing her fiery red bra. Glancing down, her eyes widened. A baseball-size mark covered the top of her breast. The deep purple bruise faded to red at the edges.

With a gentle hand, Chris probed the site. Katy hissed.

"How deep is the pain?"

"It feels like it's on the surface. When I move, the pain is in the flesh, not the bone." She'd broken ribs before. That was a pain one didn't forget.

He nodded. "You can put your shirt back on." He picked up his pen and made some notations on the chart. "You still should get some x-rays to be safe, but I think you're right. It's just a deep contusion. Do you want us to transport you to the hospital?"

"No. I'll take myself. I need to get back to the station and make some calls first." She needed to find a counselor for Misty.

"Okay. But make sure you go. You need a doctor's clearance before you can go back in the field."

Which was another reason she was glad she didn't break anything. Scheduling for extended absences when they were already understaffed was a nightmare. She vowed then and there to take home the pile of applicants for her open deputy positions tonight.

"You should put some ice on that too." He reached into a cupboard and took out a cold pack, handing it to her.

Swinging her legs over the bed, she took the cold pack, then picked up her vest and uniform shirt and stood. "Thanks for the workup."

He nodded. "Take care, Sheriff."

Katy smiled and left the ambulance, heading for her car. Climbing inside, she set her things on the passenger seat and picked up her water bottle, taking a hearty drink. Her eyes landed on her phone, and she groaned. Jasper. She needed to call him and tell him they needed to completely reschedule.

She picked up the device to see she had a missed call from him. He didn't leave a voicemail, but he sent her a text. It started with a frowning emoji, then said he understood and told her to be safe.

Touching the phone icon at the top of the text screen, she lifted it to her ear. It rang twice before his deep voice came over the line.

"Hey. Are you finished with your call?"

"Not exactly." She sighed, hating to do this to him. "It went a little sideways. We're going to have to reschedule."

"Okay. What happened? Are you all right?"

"I'm fine. A few bruises, but I've got some calls to make yet and the incident paperwork to write up."

"Bruises? Did the suspect fight you?" His voice dropped to a low growl.

She could picture the scowl on his face. Katy debated not telling him the whole truth, but immediately dismissed the idea. For one, lying was never good in a relationship, and two, he'd hear about it soon enough. It was hard to keep secrets in Pine Ridge. "He did. He also shot me."

"What!"

"He hit me in the vest, and it was only a twenty-two. I'm fine, I swear. Just a big bruise."

"Jesus, Katy. Where are you?"

"I'm still at the scene, but I'm getting ready to drive back to the station."

"Okay. I'll see you there." He hung up before she could protest.

For a millisecond, she debated calling him back, but she knew she'd never talk him out of coming. Sighing, she picked up the cold pack, stuffing it under her shirt and tucking a corner of it into her bra to hold it into place. Buckling her seatbelt and adjusting it so it was comfortable over her chest, she started the engine and drove back to town.

THIRTY

Jasper's tires gave a short squeal as he braked, coming to a stop in a parking spot outside the sheriff's department. He'd driven much faster than he probably should have into town, but the concern gnawing at his gut wouldn't let him slow down. Until he saw for himself that Katy was all right, he wouldn't relax.

Leaving his truck, he jogged toward the entrance. The deputy at the desk recognized him and shoved the visitor's log and a badge through the slot in the plexiglass.

"She just got back," the man said. "She's in her office."

Jasper scrawled his name on the log and took the badge. "Thanks." The door buzzed, and he pushed through, pinning the badge to his shirt as he hurried down the hall to Katy's office.

Outside her door, he could hear the murmur of her voice through the wood. She had the blinds drawn over her window, so he couldn't see her, but he assumed she was on the phone. But he didn't care. Twisting the knob, he opened the door. He needed to see her.

She glanced at him, holding up a finger, then pointed to

the chair in front of her desk. He sank into it, propping a foot over his knee. It bounced as he listened to her talk to whoever was on the other end of the line about meeting with the victim of her domestic violence case. She wrote down some information on a small notepad, then thanked the person and hung up.

"Before you say anything, I really am fine." She held up a hand.

His brows dipped. "You still got shot. Physically, you might be, but what about up here?" He pointed to his head. He knew he'd be reeling if he took a bullet to the chest—even wearing a vest.

"I'm sure it'll hit me later, but right now, I have too much other stuff to focus on."

He stood, rounding her desk. Spinning her chair around, he dropped to his knees in front of her, cradling her face in his hands. Words escaped him as he stared at her. His hands shook.

"Jasper." She covered his hands with hers. "I'm okay."

He pulled in a breath through his nose, nodding. "You know, I'm beginning to dislike your job. When we were on our way to Salt Lake and you subdued that suspect at the gas station, I was impressed. But when I found out he had a knife, it bothered me that you willingly put yourself in danger."

"Wait." She frowned. "That's why you were upset afterward?"

He nodded. "I told myself you were trained to handle those situations and did my best to put it out of my mind. Now, you've been shot, and I—" He broke off and shook his head. "I'm having a hard time with this. I don't want to lose you. Not to some asshole who thinks it's okay to hurt others. Hell, I don't want to lose you at all."

Her amber gaze held his, eyes widening at his words.

"Jazz, you're not going to lose me. Today was a freak thing.

I've never been shot on the job before. This is only the second time someone's ever even pulled a gun on me since I've been with the department. And Johnny O'Toole is going to jail for a long time. Please don't worry about me. I know what I'm doing and how to take care of myself."

"I can't help but worry about you, Katy." His feelings for her made his heart ache, they were so strong. He couldn't hold back the words anymore, even if she wasn't ready to hear them. "I love you. The idea of life without you—I don't want to think about it."

Her eyes grew larger, and her voice came out as a mere whisper. "What?"

His face softened with a tender smile. He leaned in to press his forehead to hers. "I love you."

She leaned back to give him a wide-eyed stare.

The smile on his face dimmed at the deer-in-headlights look on her face. "I know it's probably too soon—and we can still take things as slow as you want—but I wanted you to know I'm in this for the long haul. And I want you to understand why I don't like that you put yourself in danger. It's not that I don't think you're capable—I've seen you in action, so I know that's not the case. It's because I don't want to live without you."

A shimmer entered her eyes. "I don't know what to say."

His stomach sank, and he let his hands fall to her shoulders. He'd been hoping she'd feel the same way.

Her eyes went wide again. "Oh! No! I didn't mean it like that. Honestly, I don't know how I feel about you. I know I enjoy being with you, and I look forward to our time together. Our phone calls and texts. It all makes me happy and helps wash away the stress of this job. I can forget about being a cop, being the sheriff, when I'm with you. But I've been concentrating so much on whether we can make this work, I forgot to think about—or recognize—how you make me feel."

"It's not that hard, Katy. What does your heart say?"

She took his face in her hands. "That you're amazing, and I'm a lucky woman." She tipped her head to stare at him. "And it's not so simple as saying yes, I love you too. My feelings for you are tangled up in my fears about whether I can make a relationship work long-term. I know I've never felt what I feel for you for any other man."

Some of the hope rekindled in his chest. He knew it was a gamble to tell her how he felt at this stage. She'd been very upfront about taking things slow. About needing time to figure out her feelings. He was happy she'd made some progress, even if it wasn't exactly what he wanted to hear.

He leaned forward again to press a kiss to her lips. "I'll take it," he said, pulling back.

A bright smile bloomed on her face. Jasper smiled back, kissed her again, then stood, going back to his chair. Their nearness was messing with his ability to think. He needed the distance to gather himself. "So, what exactly happened?"

She spun back to the desk, propping her elbows on the surface, scrubbing her hands over her face. "I got there fully intending to stay outside until my backup arrived. But three of the kids were outside and told me their dad had a gun and had knocked out their oldest brother when he stepped in front of his mom. When I looked through the window, he was waving the weapon at Misty and the two kids who were still inside. I couldn't wait to defuse the situation. I thought I had him, but Misty was so angry that he hit Mikey, she kept contradicting and rebuking him." She shook her head, letting her arms drop to cross on the desk.

"He finally had enough, and because my gun and I were in the way of him harming her, I got shot. I'm glad he was drunk. I think if he was sober, he'd have aimed elsewhere."

Jasper suppressed a shudder at the thought. He knew how lucky she was to be alive.

"I fell back against the wall, and he turned, aiming at Misty, but my backup got close enough we could hear the sirens. He turned back to me, intending to shoot me again. I just reacted. I tackled him, then ended up tasing him. Ray showed up just as I got him subdued."

Pride swelled in Jasper's chest, drowning out some of the fear. His woman was a real badass. "Remind me never to fight you."

She gave a soft laugh. "It helped that he was drunk. His reaction time was slow."

He rolled his lips in, pressing them together. "I'm not going to ask you to never do anything like that again, because I know you'll do whatever's necessary. Just promise me you'll always be careful."

"That's an easy promise to make. I have no desire to see Heaven yet."

The ache in Jasper's heart pulsed again. "Good." He leaned forward, resting his elbows on his knees. "So, when do I get to take you home? I'm assuming you have work left to do?"

She nodded. "Yeah. I called a domestic violence counselor about Misty and got her permission to pass on her info." She gestured to the notepad. "I need to write up my incident report, then I'm going to head over to the hospital. I want to check on Mikey, give this info to Misty, and get an x-ray, so I'm not stuck behind a desk for the foreseeable future."

"Okay." He sat back, crossing an ankle over his knee. "Get busy."

A furrow appeared between her eyebrows. "What?"

"I'm not going anywhere, Katydid. Write your report. I'll drive you to the hospital when you're done, then take you home."

"I can drive myself, Jazz."

"I know."

She huffed, but relented. "Fine."

Her tone was gruff, but he saw the smile quirk her lips as she turned to her computer. "Do you think you could make yourself useful and instead of just sitting there staring at me, bring me some painkillers and a cup of coffee?" Her smile grew as she glanced at him.

Jasper dropped his foot to the floor and stood. He could see the pain in her eyes behind the smile. "Sure. Where's your first-aid stuff?"

"There's a cabinet in the break room with all that stuff. Coffee machine is in there too."

He picked up her mug from her desk. "I'll be right back."

"Thanks, Jasper." Weariness colored her voice.

She didn't know it, but she was getting the full pamper treatment when he got her home.

THIRTY-ONE

Mind floating and her eyes closed, it took Katy a moment to realize the truck stopped. She blinked, sitting up. Her house filled her vision, and she realized Jasper had pulled into her driveway in front of her cruiser. She frowned at the car. "How did that get here?"

He glanced at her, then at where she pointed. "Your car? I saw Deputy Hughes on my way back from the break room earlier. He asked how you were, and I told him sore and tired, and that I was taking you to the hospital for x-rays and then home. He said he'd make sure your cruiser made it back here. He also said to tell you that no one would bother you until you were ready to come in tomorrow, unless it was something only you could handle."

"Oh." She'd have to text him and thank him. When she agreed to let Jasper be her chauffeur, her only concern was how she would get her personal car and her cruiser home when she drove her car to work tomorrow. And it would be nice to not have to worry about her phone ringing unless it was a true emergency. To not be on call for once.

Pulling on the door handle, she got out of the truck and

headed for the front door. She unlocked it and let them in, flipping on the lights and dumping her things on the entryway table. A small measure of peace settled over her as Jasper shut the door. It was good to be home and in her own space.

"Go sit down in the living room. I'll get you some water and put your food on a plate and bring it in."

They'd stopped for burgers on their way home from the hospital. Katy wasn't all that hungry, but knew she needed to eat.

She nodded and turned toward the cluster of furniture on her right. Jasper headed for the kitchen.

Katy sank onto the couch, wincing slightly, but not because of her chest. Her back was killing her. Stress and fatigue had made the muscles tight.

A plate appeared in front of her face. She glanced up. "Thanks." Taking the plate, she set it on her lap. Jasper sank down beside her. He put two bottles of water on the coffee table, then sat back and picked up his burger, taking a bite.

Katy lifted a fry to her mouth. The salty goodness hit her tongue and suddenly, she was ravenous. She lifted her sandwich and took a huge bite.

Jasper chuckled. "Hungrier than you thought?"

"Apparently so." She took another bite. Now she wished she'd opted for ice cream too. Vanilla soft-serve sounded amazing. Her forehead wrinkled as she tried to remember if she had any ice cream in her freezer. It wouldn't be the same, but it would come close.

"Why are you frowning?"

"Huh?" She snapped out of her thoughts. "Oh. I was trying to remember if I had any ice cream."

He laughed. "You really are hungry. Do you want me to go check?"

She waved a hand. "Not yet. Finish your food first." A grin lit her face.

He rolled his eyes and chuckled. "Yes, ma'am. And for future reference, you may call me Jenkins."

Katy laughed. "Will you wear the suit pants and just the bow tie as your butler outfit?"

He waggled his eyebrows. "I'll wear whatever you want."

Heat blazed a trail through her as the image of Jasper in nothing but a pair of pants that hugged his tight butt entered her mind. She longed to see his naked chest again. To touch it.

The smile slowly left his face as he held her gaze. "Dammit, Katy. Don't look at me like that."

Her cheeks heated, but she couldn't look away if she wanted to. Which she didn't. Instead, she leaned closer. "Don't look at you like what?"

"You know like what," he growled through clenched teeth. "Tonight is not the night for us to take our relationship to the next level. I don't want to hurt you."

She wanted to contradict him, but her back twinged as she shifted, reminding her he was right. Grimacing, she nodded. "Quit looking so sexy."

A quick laugh burst from his chest. "I'll try."

Giggling, she picked up another fry.

He ate the last of his food and got up. "I'm going to go fill the tub for you. Finish eating?"

She nodded.

Giving her a soft smile, he walked away. Katy's eyes followed him, lingering on his tight rear. What was wrong with her? She'd been shot, and her back seized anytime she shifted a certain way, but all she wanted to do was strip him naked and ride him until the sun came up. It wasn't abnormal for her to feel that way, but she usually had better control over the urge by reminding herself they were taking things slow.

His words from earlier echoed through her mind. Were they really? He was in love with her. If the feelings rattling around in her heart were any indication, she was falling for him too. Their goodnight kisses had been increasingly longer and hotter. Was it really surprising she wanted to jump his bones? Particularly after the adrenaline-inducing evening she'd had?

But he was right. Her body wouldn't tolerate sex well tonight. She was too sore. But it was going to happen soon. Very soon.

THIRTY-TWO

Jasper turned on the water in Katy's big garden tub and squirted a healthy dose of her peach-scented bubble bath into the water. Steam filled the room as the tub filled. He found a towel in the cabinet and put it within her reach.

Satisfied things were ready for her, he headed back to the great room. Katy was in the kitchen, putting her plate in the dishwasher. As he neared, she reached for the dishes in the sink.

"Freeze."

She glanced back.

He walked toward her and put his hands on her shoulders, pulling her away from the counter. "I'll do the dishes. You are going to get in the tub."

Her eyes said she wanted to argue, but she wisely nodded and let him lead her from the room. They walked down the hall to her bedroom and went through to her en suite.

She stopped by the tub, staring down at the growing mound of bubbles, then turned watery eyes on him.

He frowned, reaching out to wipe away a tear with his

thumb. "Why are you crying? Do you need more pain medicine?" Maybe he should take her back to the hospital. The x-rays were negative for breaks, but that didn't mean she didn't need stronger painkillers.

"No," she whispered. "I'm okay." She sniffed. "I'm just thankful. For you. Thank you for taking care of me. I know I fight it, but I'm just not used to it." She wiped at her face. "It's very nice, though."

Jasper tugged her into his body and wrapped his arms around her. "Well, get used to it, because I'm not going anywhere." He squeezed her, pressing a kiss to her temple.

She squeaked and pushed against his hold.

"Sorry!" He let go.

"It's okay." She put a hand over her chest. "It doesn't hurt too much when I move, but when you push against it—ouch."

"How big is the bruise?" He glanced at her hand.

"Last I looked, it was about the size of a baseball." She grimaced. "It might have grown, though. It's been a bit. I tried not to look when the doctor examined me. I didn't want to think about it. About what could have been."

Jasper didn't either. He swallowed around the sudden lump in his throat and put his hand over hers. Their eyes met, and he reached up to pull the hair-tie from her hair. It flowed down around her shoulders. He thrust his hand into the blonde curtain and fanned it out. She closed her eyes and leaned into his touch.

He dipped his head, brushing his lips along her jawline. Her breath puffed against his cheek. Desire curled in his belly, and he pulled back. "Take your bath. I'll stay until you're ready for bed, if you want."

Her steady gaze studied his face. "Will you stay all night?"

His eyes widened. "Um." He swallowed, then forced

himself to breathe. She didn't mean it the way his body wanted her to. Did she? "I'm not sure that's a great idea."

She brushed her fingers against his chest. "Please? I—don't want to be alone tonight."

The emotion and the unspoken admission that she needed him made his decision an easy one. "Okay. I'll stay."

THIRTY-THREE

Katy jolted as her brain registered that she was falling asleep in the tub again. Heaving a sigh, she sat up and reached for the drain. She let the water out, sitting in it a bit longer, not wanting to leave its warmth. But it quickly lowered, exposing her to the air.

She grumbled to herself as she stood and reached for her towel. She didn't want to get out, but she needed to go to bed. With quick movements, she wrapped the towel around her body, fastening it as loosely as she could over her breasts, so she didn't put pressure on her injury. The heat had brought out the color in the contusion. It was nearly black now, with pockets of blue dotting it before it faded to red at the edges.

Stepping over to the sink, she brushed her teeth, then wandered out into the bedroom to find some pajamas. She took a loose t-shirt, a pair of panties, and some cotton shorts from her dresser and slipped them on. She let her hair out of the bun she'd scraped it into for her bath and laid the hair-tie on the dresser.

Her eyes landed on the bed as she turned to leave. Jasper had put her vest, gun belt, and uniform shirt on the bed. She walked over, securing her gun in the nightstand, and hung the belt over the corner of the wingback chair by the window. Going back to the bed, she picked up her shirt and vest.

The hole in the vest caught her attention. Yellow fibers peeked out. She knew the bullet was gone. A crime scene tech met her at the hospital and dug it out to put it into evidence. But she could still feel it. Feel the hard, flattened metal embedded in the fabric, still hot from the gun, beneath her fingertips.

She drew in a sharp breath through her nose. It left her lungs just as fast, catching in her throat on its way out. A tear leaked from her eye, and she sank onto the bed. The sob she'd held back burst free as her mind finally caught up to the evening's events and realized just how close she'd come to dying. Again.

Katy didn't know how long she sat there crying before Jasper came in and wrapped her in his strong arms. She turned her face into his chest and clutched fistfuls of his shirt as she let out all the pain and fear. He stroked her hair and rocked her gently while she soaked his shirt with her tears. She leaned into his strength and let it soothe her until finally she could lift her head again.

"Feel better?"

Sniffing, she nodded.

"Wanna talk about it?"

Her mouth twisted. "Not really."

His expression shuttered. Katy pushed back a sigh of frustration with herself. Why did she find it so hard to open up about her feelings? It wasn't like she'd ever been in a bad relationship where her partner exploited her emotions.

She sat up, but left her hands pressed against his chest. Fiddling with a button on his shirt, she gathered her thoughts into words. "I'm not sure why it's hard for me to talk about how I feel." She chanced a glance at him. His expression softened at her words, giving her courage to continue. "I think it might have something to do with my profession. In the military, strength and mental toughness were prized above most everything else. And as an MP, I had to be tough. Both mentally and with the people with whom I interacted. You can't walk a search grid looking for IEDs and not compartmentalize your emotions. Plus, as a woman, any sign of a softer emotion often gets me ridiculed." She couldn't count the number of times she'd heard she shouldn't be a cop because she was a woman. That she was too soft. So, she buried a lot of what she felt in an attempt to get people to see her—and respect her—like they did her male counterparts.

Jasper covered her hand on his chest with his, tangling their fingers together. Katy kept her eyes on their clasped hands and continued. "My tears weren't all about today. The shooting brought back memories." She paused, taking a shaky breath.

"Of what ended your military career?"

She nodded.

"What happened?" His voice was soft.

Katy let go of his hand and climbed further onto the bed. Settling against the headboard, she grabbed a pillow and clutched it against her stomach. Jasper moved up to sit beside her. He didn't take her hand again, but sat close enough their shoulders touched. She leaned into his side, borrowing a bit of his strength.

"We were on patrol ahead of a visit from one of the generals. My unit was sent out to sweep for IEDs along his route. The road was fine, so we continued into the village he wanted to visit on his way to the base. It was there we ran into a mess. I got my dog, Kaz, out to aid in the sweep. We were on our fourth public building when gunfire erupted. Two of my teammates went down right away, and I took a shot to the back. My vest stopped it."

"Oh, man." Jasper's arm went around her.

She shifted, tucking into his side and putting a hand on his abdomen. "I didn't stay down long, even though I couldn't breathe. Bullets still flew around me. Kaz and I ducked into an alley out of the line of fire. Once I caught my breath, we ran down it. I was hoping to come up on the other side of the shooters." Her voice caught on the emotion gathering in her throat. She swallowed and blinked back more tears. "I went around the end of the alley toward the shooter. The other three members of my team were ten yards away, firing into a house. I could see muzzle flashes coming from the window as the guy shot back."

Katy picked at a piece of lint on his shirt. "I remember hearing a child crying. It was a little boy, standing out front of the house next to the shooter's on my side. He'd been playing with a soccer ball when the firefight started."

Jasper's hand curled around her shoulder and squeezed.

"As my brain registered the shootout and the child so close by, another man stepped out of the house behind us all, holding a pipe bomb. Kaz yanked the leash from my hand and charged him. I dove toward the kid, but barely made it two steps when the guy threw it into the middle of us."

"Dear God, Katy." His arm tightened.

She curled her fingers into his shirt, bunching the fabric. "Everyone died, including the bomber and the kid and my dog. Everyone was just gone. Except me." She squeezed her eyes shut against the memory. Of the boy's bloodied, lifeless body on the ground in front of her.

Tears leaked out to run down her face in hot, wet tracks. "The shrapnel hit me in my back and legs. The blast was off to my left, which is why that leg and side took the brunt of the damage. I found out later the bomb was full of nails and ball bearings. I got lucky I wasn't hurt worse, but I was just far enough away and my gear handled the explosion like it was supposed to. All my injuries were just below the line of my vest and down my legs. It shattered both bones in my lower left leg and broke my right tibia in two spots. I also had extensive damage to the muscles in my lower back, and some of the shrapnel penetrated deep enough to nick my spine as well as damage the nerves in my hip and butt. I remember lying on the ground on my stomach, staring at the dirt in shock. The pain hadn't hit yet. My ears were ringing. When I tried to push myself up, that's when I realized something was wrong with my back and legs. I didn't get a chance to think much of it, though. The shooter ran out of the house with his gun. He went to my teammates and shot them, one-by-one, to make sure they were dead. I knew I was next."

The breath froze in her lungs. She swallowed hard and continued. "I somehow got my rifle around and got a shot off before he could fire." She closed her eyes, the image of the man's face burned into her brain. As long as she lived, she would never forget the surprise in his eyes or the sight of the life draining from them as he dropped to the ground, dead almost instantly from her shot that went straight through his heart.

She sniffed again and wiped the tears from her face, then glanced up at him. "When I came back, people called me a hero." She shook her head and looked away. "I'm not a hero. I just defended myself."

Jasper soothed the hair away from her face. "You are a hero, Katydid. You ran toward danger. And your first thought as you registered that danger was to save a child, not yourself. That's what makes you heroic—knowing you could die, but doing it anyway. Stopping the shooter, that was instinct. But putting yourself in front of a bomb to save a kid? That's courage."

"Maybe." She pulled in a breath and blew it out slowly,

trying to wrangle her emotions back into their box. The lid was gone, but she was hoping to at least corral them.

"No. Not maybe. Yes." He put a finger under her chin and tipped her face up.

Katy stared into his beautiful gray eyes. Their steely depths shone with unshed tears.

"You're amazing, and I love you more now than I did five minutes ago, knowing what you went through. People sink into depression and PTSD for less. But you haven't. You're strong and capable. Successful. I understand now why the commissioners chose you as sheriff."

A soft snort passed her lips. "I had both. It took years of therapy and sheer willpower to conquer them. Sometimes— like now—they still rear their ugly heads, especially the PTSD."

"I get that. But you're not alone in dealing with it. I think you know that now, yes? Which is why you're telling me all this?"

She nodded. "Yeah. I realized if we're going to have a future, I have to share all of myself with you. You deserve that."

"We both do." He pressed a soft kiss to her mouth.

Katy ran her hand up his chest to curl around the side of his neck. His hair tickled her fingers as she kissed him back. More emotions clambered their way out of their box, but these were different from the ones she just stuffed back in. They were happy ones. And she was content to let them out to play.

He gentled the kiss, breaking it off to give her a soft smile. "Thank you for sharing that with me."

She returned his smile and laid her cheek against his chest. "You're welcome. Thank you for being here. You've made what happened tonight easier to deal with."

Jasper hugged her tight. "Anytime, Katydid."

The gruffness in his voice did something to her insides. Her heart thudded in her chest, and she blinked back tears. She still couldn't name what she felt. She was too jumbled up from the roller coaster of her day. But she knew whatever was happening between them was the real deal.

Spent from her confession and the purge of all the pain she'd kept bottled up, fatigue stole over her, taking away any chance she had of deciphering her feelings for Jasper. Her brain refused to deal with anything else. Darkness crowded the edges of her mind as it shut down.

Katy took a deep breath, filling her head with Jasper's scent. It calmed the last bits of her mind and cleared the way for sleep to take her away.

THIRTY-FOUR

"Okay. I've got you on my calendar. I look forward to meeting you." Katy clicked out of the calendar app on her computer and said goodbye to the person on the phone. She'd just scheduled the last interview for the two open deputy positions.

Smiling, she glanced around her office. She needed some fresh air. Hell, what she really needed was a day off. And why not? It was a Saturday, and the weather was beautiful. Ray kept telling her he could take calls if she needed some time. He'd tried to get her to take last weekend off, but Katy wanted to make sure all the paperwork to keep Johnny in jail for a very long time was perfect. No uncrossed "t" or undotted "i" was going to keep him from getting what he deserved.

She had gone in late, though. After she fell asleep in Jasper's arms, she'd slept like the dead. A few nightmares roused her in the middle of the night, but Jasper's big body next to hers helped her fall right back to sleep. They'd enjoyed a leisurely late breakfast together before he went home. She went into the office after that, and since she was there anyway, she took a couple call outs when things got busy. Ray had been shaking his head at her all week.

Picking up the phone again, she called him. It rang three times in her ear before he answered.

"Katy. Is everything okay?"

"Things are fine. Were you serious about taking my on-call time?"

"Well, yeah. Wait, are you actually going to take a day off?"

She knew by the surprise in his tone she didn't do it often enough. That was something she was hoping to change once she got through the interviews and picked two new deputies. "Yes, I want to take a day off. Today, actually. Are you free to cover for me?"

"Yeah, sure. I'm just puttering around the house. Monica has me working on my honey-do list. Trust me when I say I'd love to put it off."

Katy chuckled. "Okay. Well, tell her I said you had to work. That should save your hide."

He laughed, shocking Katy. It was a rare sound from her chief deputy.

"No need. Once I tell her you want to take a day off, she'll hand me my gun and shove me out the door herself."

"If you say so. But still apologize for me for halting the progress on her list."

"I will. Contact dispatch and have them transfer your calls to me. You should take tomorrow off too. I'll see you Monday."

"Oh." She sat up. Tomorrow hadn't even crossed her mind. But she liked the idea. "Are you sure?"

He sighed, the sound exasperated. "Yes."

She chuckled again. "Okay, okay. I'll see you Monday. Thanks, Ray."

"Of course. Have a good weekend."

"I will. Bye." He echoed her goodbye, and she hung up.

She stared at the phone in its cradle. What was she going to do all weekend?

Jasper's face entered her mind. She owed him a date. And a good one. He'd told her about the one they'd had to cancel. She hoped they got another chance to do that. It sounded fun. In the meantime, she'd make it up to him. Glancing at the clock, she noted the time. She had a good idea how to start.

Pushing away from her desk, she took her purse from her desk drawer and left her office, heading outside to her cruiser. A quick trip later, she pulled into the parking lot at Sarafina's. The bell tinkled over the door as she entered.

"Hey, Katy. How are you?" The diner's owner, Sara Katsaros, smiled at her from behind the long counter.

"I'm great." Katy returned her smile and took a seat. "How about you?"

"Can't complain."

"Good. How's James? How's his book coming along?" Sara's fiancé, James O'Malley, was a best-selling thriller author. Katy loved his books.

Sara rolled her eyes. "Better than he thinks. He finished the first one in the series in no time. He's on book two, but it's not going as fast because we've been wedding planning. He keeps telling me I distract him." A wicked smile crossed her face. "Which I do, but he likes it, so he needs to stop bitching."

Katy barked out a laugh.

Grinning, Sara leaned her hands on the counter. "So, what can I get you?"

"Can you make a picnic lunch for me?"

"A picnic?" Sara frowned, then her expression cleared and she grinned. "For you and a certain handsome ranch hand?"

Katy returned her smile. "Yep."

"I sure can. What would you like?"

"Whatever would keep well. I want to run home and

change yet before I head out there. Depending on what he's doing, we might not eat right away, either."

Sara gave a short nod. "How about fried chicken, coleslaw, and some pie? You put some ice packs around it and the chicken will keep. And it's delicious cold."

"That sounds great."

"Okay. Give me a few minutes."

Katy nodded. "Can I have a Diet Coke while I wait?"

"Yep." Sara spun around and picked up a glass from the stacks behind her. She filled it with ice, then pushed it against the lever on the soda machine, filling it with the dark brown liquid.

"There you go." She set it in front of Katy and handed her a straw.

"Thanks." Katy peeled the paper off and stuck it in the drink as Sara smiled and pushed through the doors to the kitchen. She perched a hip on a bar stool and turned, glancing over the customers. The diner was only half full. It was still a little early for lunch.

While she waited, she scrolled through her email—the one thing she hadn't done yet today that she normally did. Thankfully, nothing pressing had landed in her inbox since yesterday.

The kitchen door swung open. Katy looked up to see Sara come through carrying a plastic sack. She put the bag on the counter, then reached beneath for two clear clamshell containers.

"What kind of pie do you want?"

"I'll take peach. I'm not sure what kind Jasper likes. Do you know?"

"He likes peach too." She opened the pie case and scooped two pieces of peach pie into the containers, then put them in the sack along with two sets of plastic silverware and some extra napkins. "I added some dinner rolls too. They're in their own box."

"Oh, great. Thank you."

"Sure." She rang Katy up at the register, then passed the bag and receipt to her with a playful smile. "Have fun."

Katy grinned. "I plan to. Thanks." With a small wave, she left the diner and headed home.

As quickly as she could, she changed into jeans, a t-shirt, and a pair of boots. She packed all the food, plus two waters, into a soft-sided cooler, grabbed a lightweight hoodie, then left again.

Rolling all the windows down, she cranked up the radio and sang along as she wound her way through the mountains to the Stone Creek. For the first time in a long time, Katy felt free of her demons. They were still there—and always would be—but sharing them with Jasper helped her shoulder the burden.

She was also happy, she realized. After her military career ended, she hadn't tried to truly engage with life again. It hurt too much when it was all ripped away. But he got under her skin like a precision blade. Quick and mostly painless. But he didn't leave a gaping hole in his wake. The opposite, actually. He'd filled a place she didn't know needed filled. Now, she wanted more than just her job to fill her days. She wanted a family of her own. She wanted Jasper.

Love sucker-punched her in the gut, stealing her breath. Her eyes widened and her heart beat faster. The music faded as blood rushed through her ears. She let off the gas, slowing the car as her mind tried to catch up to the feelings flooding her.

"Oh my God," she breathed. A smile wreathed her face. "Oh my God." She couldn't stop the bright laugh that filled the car.

Her mind caught up, she pressed the gas pedal again, trying not to speed the rest of the way.

THIRTY-FIVE

"Jasper!"

Asa's shout made Jasper look up. He glanced back to see his boss—and friend—headed toward him on his horse, Storm.

Straightening from tightening the piece of wire around the fence, he poked the brim of his hat, pushing it higher on his forehead. Man and horse came to a halt a few feet away.

"Everything okay?"

Asa nodded. "Yeah. You have a visitor."

"Oh. Why didn't you just call me?"

"I tried. You didn't answer."

"What?" He took his phone from his pocket and saw several missed calls. His frown cleared when he remembered he forgot to take it off silent mode when he got up this morning. "Sorry. I forgot to turn the sound back on." He looked up. "Who's here?"

"Katy."

"Katy? She said she had to work. Why is she here?" A terrifying thought slammed into him, making sweat break out on his forehead and palms, and his heartbeat quicken. "Is Megan okay?"

"As far as I know. She's not here on business, Jazz. She brought you lunch."

"Lunch?"

"Yes, lunch, you damn parrot." Asa got off his horse. "Get your ass on your horse and go see your girl. I'll finish this section of fence. You don't need to be out here, anyway. When was the last time you took a day off?"

A corner of Jasper's mouth ticked up as he handed Asa his wire cutters. He didn't give Katy as much grief as he could about taking time off because he was a workaholic himself. "I guess I'm taking one today."

"Yes, you are. Go. Have fun. Oh, and Daisy said to tell you not to run her off, because she wants more friends."

Jasper laughed and mounted Castle. "Tell her I'm glad, because I plan for Katy to be around a good long time." He wheeled his horse around and took off for home.

Katy waited for him in the barn. He rode in to see her leaning against Castle's stall door.

"Hi." He grinned down at her from atop his horse.

She returned his easy smile with a sassy one of her own. "Hi."

"Asa said you brought me lunch."

"I did."

He laid his hands over the pommel of his saddle, striking a casual pose. "And what is it that warrants such an action? And your attire?" He narrowed his eyes, taking in her t-shirt and jeans, with the gray hoodie tied around her waist and the leather boots on her feet. "Did you—did you take a day off?"

She laughed, the merry sound warming Jasper's heart. He'd never seen her quite so carefree.

"I did. I took two."

His eyes widened. "What?"

"Two." She held up two fingers, wiggling them, and pushed away from the wall, coming to stand next to him. Laying a hand on his thigh, her smile turned heated. "How about you put the horse wherever he needs to go and see what I brought for lunch?"

An answering heat lit in his blood. He leaned down to put his face close to hers. "I can't."

She pulled back, frowning. "What? Why?"

"You're in the way." His gaze flicked past her to the stall at her back.

Laughing, she rolled her eyes, then stood on her toes to give him a brief kiss. "Go. Take care of your horse. I'll go get the food."

"Wait." He laid a hand over hers on his thigh. "Is it something we can take with us?"

"Actually, yes. I wanted to have a picnic, but I figured we could do that in the ranch yard somewhere."

He smiled. "I have a better spot. Can your back and leg handle a horseback ride?"

Katy nodded. "So long as it isn't too far."

"It's not. Maybe half an hour or so."

"Okay. That sounds fun."

Jasper dismounted and tied Castle to the cleat on the wall. "I'll saddle you a horse. You don't have too much experience on horseback, do you?"

"No."

"You can ride Daisy's horse, Patches, then. He's gentle. Want to help me?"

"Sure."

"Let's go." He led her down the corridor to the tack room to get Daisy's saddle and Patches' bridle, swinging by the horse's stall on the way. He saddled the horse outside the tack room, then left him with her to retrieve Castle.

"I need to get the food from my car. It's just outside the barn." She pointed toward the main door.

"I'll meet you in the corral around back."

They split up. Jasper led the horses down the aisle and out the back of the barn. Katy rounded the side of the building a few moments later, carrying a cooler that looked like a large fabric lunch box. He took it from her, tying a knot in the long strap to loop it over his saddle horn.

"You ready?" He glanced at her.

"Yep." She put her left foot in the stirrup. "Let's see if I can still do this and not fall backward."

Jasper chuckled and stood behind her. "I'll catch you."

She tossed him a grin and pulled herself up, swinging her other leg over to straddle the horse's back.

"Are the stirrups a good length?" He looked at her leg. She was only an inch or so taller than Daisy, so they should be fine.

Katy rose up to stand in them. "They're fine." She sank back down.

"Good." He turned to Castle, then paused. "Oh! I almost forgot. I'll be right back." He dashed into the barn to the supply room where they kept the gear they used for overnight roundups. Snatching a rolled blanket from a tub on the shelf, he jogged back outside.

He held it up as he approached. "Ground cover."

"Oh. I didn't even think about that. I don't mind the grass."

"Where we're going, you will. It's scrub grass, so it's prickly." He tied it to the back of his saddle, then mounted up. "Okay. I think we're ready."

"Lead the way."

Jasper led her through the corral gate into the yard and headed for the hills, away from where Asa fixed the fencing. The spot he had in mind was out of view of the ranch buildings.

"So, what made you take two days off?" Jasper asked after they'd settled into the ride.

"The weather."

He arched an eyebrow. "How so?"

"I scheduled interviews this morning for my two open deputy positions. After I ended the last call, I decided I needed some fresh air. But I wanted more than a few minutes. Ray's been harping on me to take some time—that he'd cover for me—so I finally took him up on it. I only wanted today, but he offered tomorrow too. I was only going to put a few hours in patrolling in the morning, then stay on call the rest of the day, anyway. So, unless something crazy happens, I'm off until Monday."

"You know, I'm not sure we know what to do with all that time."

She chuckled. "I know. But I'm sure we can think of something."

The fire that leapt to life in her eyes told him exactly what she thought that something should be. He wasn't going to argue with her. He shifted in his saddle, trying to put a little more space between his crotch and the saddle horn.

They chatted as they rode, talking about the things they'd like to do this summer. He learned Katy planned to take an actual vacation once her two new deputies were fully trained. That worked for him. It had been a long time since he went anywhere not associated with search and rescue or ranching. Lazing around on a beach somewhere sounded fantastic.

Cresting a ridge, he pointed Castle down the slope to a small natural watering hole. It had a great view through the pines to the river and valley below.

"Wow! This is gorgeous." Katy got off her horse, staring at the view.

"Yeah. It's a hidden gem, that's for sure." He got down

from Castle's back. "Though I guess it's not much of a secret. We all come up here to swim in the summer. I've stopped here many times when I'm out working just to cool off." He untied the blanket and tucked it under one arm, then lifted the cooler off the saddle.

"Where should we sit?"

He shrugged. "You pick."

Katy pointed to a spot not far from the water. It was directly across from a gap in the trees. Jasper handed her the cooler, then spread the blanket on the ground.

"I don't know about you, but I'm hungry." She sank to her knees on the blanket and unzipped the cooler.

Jasper knelt next to her. "Yeah. It's past lunchtime now." He took the boxes as she handed them to him. "Oh, peach pie." His mouth watered. "You got all this at Sarafina's, didn't you?"

"Yep."

He loved her pie. All her food, really.

Once she had everything out of the bag, she handed him a set of plastic silverware. "Dig in."

Jasper opened the box with the fried chicken and picked up a drumstick, taking a bite.

"So, how's your sister? She still having problems with that boy?"

Some of Jasper's mood soured at her question. "Yes. I changed her phone number. I can't do anything about her living situation, though, until after her classes end. But even then, I'm not sure it'll keep him away. They go to the same school, and the campus isn't that large. He knows her major, so he'll know where to look for her and could follow her home."

"He still hasn't threatened her?"

"Nope. Just bothers her, begging her to take him back."

He scooped up a forkful of coleslaw into his mouth. "We talked to the cops. They told her to document all the harassment."

"At this point, she could prove stalking and get a restraining order. Especially with a statement from her roommate that he keeps showing up at their house. I can talk to her and put her in contact with the court in Billings to file the paperwork."

"Really? That would be great."

"Have her call me tonight or tomorrow. I'll walk her through the process. She can file the application online, but she'll have to appear in court to show her documentation."

A bit of the sourness receded as she offered him a sliver of hope that something could finally be done about Megan's asshole ex. He finished his coleslaw and chicken and moved on to his pie.

The first bite made him moan. "Oh, that's so good."

Katy chuckled and polished off the last of her chicken, then reached for her slice. "Sara makes the best peach pie." She ate a bite, echoing his moan.

The sound shot straight to his groin. Her earlier words about finding something to occupy them this weekend filtered through his thoughts. He set his pie aside and popped to his knees.

"Jasper?"

He moved toward her, his eyes locked on hers. "Did you know that the scent of your shampoo and bubble bath drives me insane?" He took the pie container and fork from her.

"It does?"

"Yes. You smell like peaches." He leaned closer, burying his nose in her hair near her ear. "I love peaches."

He heard her shaky breath.

"Me too."

Turning his head, he pressed a hot kiss to the spot just

behind her ear. She moaned again, making him groan. He pulled back to look into her eyes.

"We're not going to finish our pie right now, are we?"

"No." His mouth crashed onto hers, and he wrapped her in his arms.

THIRTY-SIX

Fireworks went off in Katy's brain as Jasper kissed her. She knew this moment was coming after she saw the understanding in his eyes at her comment earlier. But she figured they'd make it back to his house at least. She didn't care, though. All she wanted was him.

"We should go," he breathed against her lips.

Her fingers found the buttons on his shirt, and she popped them free from their holes. "Why?" The edges of the gray cotton parted, and she slid her hands inside over his warm skin.

He moaned. "Because I have a big, comfortable bed back at my house."

"I can't wait that long."

"Oh, thank God. Me neither." He attacked her mouth again, then immediately pulled back. "Wait."

"What?" Her wide, honeyed eyes stared at him.

"We can't."

"Why the hell not?"

"Because I don't have any protection on me. Do you?"

"No. But unless you have some disease, we don't need it. I've been on the pill for years and I'm disease free."

He framed her face in his hands. "Are you sure?"

Katy didn't bother with words. She just kissed him again. He grunted, but quickly took over the kiss. That was fine with her. It freed her to focus on other things. Like removing his shirt so she could touch his glorious chest. She pushed her hands inside, sliding them over his shoulders and down his arms. The fabric fell away. He gave his arms a shake, freeing them.

She covered his pecs with her hands, molding them to the swell of muscle and tunneling her fingers through his springy chest hair. The warm breeze hit her back as he lifted her t-shirt. Raising her arms, he rid her of the garment. Katy dove back into their kiss and let her hands drift further south over his abs. She followed the line of dark hair that split the middle, letting it lead her to the waistband of his jeans.

With fingers far more nimble than she thought they would be at this point, she unbuckled his belt, then unbuttoned and unzipped his jeans. His position resting on his legs made it hard for her to get inside them. She tore her mouth from his. "Take off your pants."

His mouth tipped up. "What happened to 'let's go slow?'"

She took his face in her hands, making sure he was looking into her eyes. "I think we're well past the slow stage now."

He grinned.

"Plus, on the way up here, I realized I was happy because I was on my way to see you." Her thumbs traced his cheekbones. "You make me happy." The words "I love you" stuck in her throat. Something kept her from saying them, but what? It wasn't like she was afraid he wouldn't say them back.

Those steely eyes held her gaze for several long beats, oblivious to her inner struggle. Love shone from their depths. A fierce determination filled them, along with hot desire. In an instant, she was on her back with him looming over her.

"I think you're right. Slow is overrated." With a quick pinch of his fingers, he opened the front clasp on her bra. As he reached for her breasts, though, he paused, his gaze landing on the still dark purple bruise on the left side of her chest. He feathered his fingers over it. Katy watched a riot of emotions cross his face. Pain, fear, sorrow, love—they were all there.

She put her hands on his. "I'm okay."

He looked at her. "I know. I won't ever stop worrying about you when you step out the door to go to work. But I'm proud of what you do. I love you, Katy."

Grabbing the sides of his face, she tugged him to her and kissed him again, letting every ounce of love she felt flow into the touch, even though the words refused to come. His hands landed on her breasts, being mindful of the tenderness from her injury. It didn't stop the instant jolt of pleasure that shot through her, though. She doubted anything could dampen that.

He rolled, so she was on top. Katy took the opportunity to stand up and remove the rest of her clothes. Naked, she stared down at him.

"Are you going to join the party or do I have to pleasure myself?"

She took great pride in watching the muscles in his belly clench and the bulge behind his exposed boxer briefs grow at her words. Growling, he pushed his pants and underwear down his legs, kicking his feet to get them off.

Her mouth dried up as she got her first look at what he'd been hiding behind his clothes. Long and thick, his erection jutted away from his body, a dot of moisture on the end. She licked her lips, wanting to taste.

"No."

"What?" Her gaze snapped to his.

"You can use that pretty mouth on me another time. I'm barely going to last as it is. Get down here." He reached up and tugged her hand, yanking her down on top of him.

Her core slid along his length, making them both moan. She was done waiting. Rising up on her knees, she grasped him and lowered herself, taking him in one smooth movement. All the breath left her body at the exquisite sensation of him stretching and filling her to the max. Jasper was a big man. Everywhere.

The burn of his invasion faded, and she lifted her hips, then lowered them down again. She only did it twice before he rolled them and took control. Katy locked her ankles behind his back. Her moans of pleasure quickly turned to a grunt of pain, though, as the ground dug into her back.

Jasper froze and looked down at her with wide eyes. "Shit, did I hurt you?"

"No. It's the ground. Maybe you were right and we should have waited."

His wide-eyed look disappeared, and a sexy smile took its place. "Nah. You just need to ride." He flipped them again.

Katy's eyes rolled up as the movement made him hit all the right spots. "Oh, I hope you're close. I won't last long like this."

"No worries, babe." He groaned, lifting his hips to grind against her.

An airy moan pushed past her lips at the lovely friction he created. Her inner walls squeezed, and he pulsed within her. He thrust up again, and she met his movement, rising and falling in time to his driving hips.

Without warning, her climax hit. More fireworks went off inside her head, brighter and more thrilling than ever before. She watched the show, letting the pleasure feed her soul as his harsh cry added to the cacophony going off inside her mind.

When the last flash of color died, she sagged against his

chest. He stroked her hair, pushing it away from her face. She smiled at him. "So, we're going to do that again on a proper bed, right?"

"Oh, hell yeah."

She traced his cheekbone with the tip of her finger, staring into his beautiful gray eyes. "Good."

THIRTY-SEVEN

"They need popcorn for this thing."

Katy snickered at Jasper as he read the playbill for the high school play. They were on a date. With her grandma. Neither of them minded, though. They'd had plenty of time together lately, just the two of them, and had settled into their relationship. She enjoyed spending time with Jasper in any way she could.

"I mean, seriously. Zombies from radioactive waste and a mean school principal? It's like Spiderman, only funnier."

"I tried to tell the school board that, but they said no." Heidi sighed next to Katy. "Too much of a hassle, they said." She snorted. "They do it for sporting events. Why can't the drama kids have it too?"

Katy agreed. But even without refreshments, they would enjoy the play. She was eager to see it.

The lights flashed with the five-minute warning, then dimmed. Katy's phone buzzed on her hip. She took it from its holder and glanced at it. It was dispatch. "I need to take this. I'll be right back."

"Everything okay?" Jasper looked up at her in concern as she stood.

"It's dispatch, so I'm not sure." She slid past him, giving his shoulder a gentle squeeze and answered the phone. "Sheriff Lattimer." She started up the aisle out of the auditorium.

"Sheriff, we have a report of an accident just past the bridge on the highway, heading away from town," the female dispatcher said.

"Okay. There are other deputies in the area. Are they all on calls?" Someone waved at her in greeting as they passed her to enter the auditorium. She gave the man a polite smile and wandered further from the crowd so she could concentrate.

"No, ma'am. Deputy Goodman responded. He asked us to contact you. It's a two-car accident, but there are no victims present."

"What? Both drivers left the scene?"

"Yes, ma'am."

"Who are the cars registered to?"

"The white Honda Pilot is registered to David and Olivia Anderson. The blue Toyota Highlander is registered to Megan Pierce."

The bottom dropped out of Katy's stomach. "Did you say Megan Pierce?" She and Jasper had done a lot of talking in the last few weeks, learning more about each other's families and pasts. One thing she'd learned was the name of Jasper's step-dad, and Megan's father: Kevin Pierce.

"Affirmative."

"Can you pull up her license information for me?" *Please be wrong.*

"Sure." The dispatcher sounded confused, but Katy still heard her typing.

"How old is she?"

"Um, twenty."

Katy cursed. "About five-nine with brown hair and blue eyes?"

"Yeah. How did you know?"

"Because I know her. It's my boyfriend's sister. Tell Goodman I'm on my way."

"Yes, ma'am." Urgency took over her voice and the line clicked as she hung up.

Katy spun around, hurrying through the throng of people walking to their seats to get to Jasper.

He glanced up as she stopped beside him. The smile on his face quickly died when he saw her expression. "What? What's wrong?"

"You need to come with me. There's been an accident out by the bridge. It's Megan."

All the color drained from his face. Katy heard her grandma gasp.

"Is she—" His voice cut off.

"I don't know. The dispatcher said she was gone. So was the driver of the other car."

He frowned. "Gone? Like missing? Why would they leave the scene without their cars? Where would they go?"

"I don't know that either. We need to get out to the scene. Maybe it'll offer some clues."

"Yeah, okay." He stood up.

"I'm sorry to run out on you, Grandma." Katy peered around him.

Heidi waved her hands. "Go. Find Megan. And keep me posted."

"I will." Katy took Jasper's hand. "Let's go."

They hurried up the aisle as the lights went out and the music swelled, signaling the start of the play. The auditorium door closed behind them, muffling the noise to almost nothing.

"You're sure it's Megan?"

They hurried down the hall to the exit.

"It's her car. It's registered to her. The other car is registered to David and Olivia Anderson."

He stopped, his boots scuffing on the floor. "Anderson?"

She glanced back at him. "Yeah. Do you know them?"

"Megan's ex. Burke. His last name is Anderson."

Katy let out another curse. She tugged on his hand, picking up the pace. If this was an abduction, time was critical. And they only had about an hour of daylight left. It would take twenty minutes to get to the accident site.

They ran outside and got into Jasper's truck. She directed him to her house, so they could get her cruiser and weapon. She was in and out in two minutes, buckling the gear belt around her waist as she ran outside.

Jasper met her at the cruiser and climbed into the passenger seat as she unlocked it. Katy hit the lights and siren and pulled out of her driveway.

As they exited town, she noticed him tapping his index finger on the window frame. His jaw worked.

"We'll find her." She covered his other hand with hers.

He turned his palm up and laced his fingers through hers. A nod was his only response.

"Can you think of why he would abduct her now?" Something had to set the kid off. He'd been harassing her, but none of his actions were violent.

"She started seeing someone new. Just a couple of dates. And she filed for a restraining order the other day. He followed her on a date with the guy and made a scene. The judge gave her a thirty-day order. We were hoping the temporary one would be enough, since it was the end of the school year. That he'd get the hint and leave her alone. I really didn't think he'd follow her up here. He knows she has an older brother, and I'm sure she told him he didn't want to mess with me."

"What's the new boyfriend's name?" She let go of his hand and reached for the radio.

Jasper looked at her hand, his eyes growing wide. "Hell. I didn't even think about him. Danny. Um, Danny Fulton." He lifted a hip to take out his phone. "Megan's roommate might know him. Let me have her try to call him before you send Billings police to his house."

She nodded and withdrew her hand. He found the number for Megan's roommate and dialed.

"Izzy, it's Jasper. Megan's brother. Do you have contact information for that guy she went out with a couple of times? Danny?" He put a finger in his ear to drown out the sound of the siren. A frown crossed his face as he listened. "No, I can't. She's missing. I think Burke is involved. I just want to check on Danny and make sure he's okay."

Katy glanced over to see his head bob. She mimed a phone to her ear, then mouthed to have Danny call him.

He nodded at her. "Great. Let me know either way. If you do get ahold of him, give him my number and tell him to call me. I think the sheriff here has some questions she wants to ask." They said goodbye, and he hung up.

Dropping his phone in his lap, he swiped a hand over his face and stared out the window. Katy eyed the darkening skies. They weren't going to get much of a search started before dark. She edged the speedometer needle a little higher.

As they neared the accident site, Jasper's phone rang.

"I don't recognize the number. It's probably Danny."

"Put it on speaker."

He answered it, holding it between them. "Hello?"

"Hi. Um, this is Danny Fulton. Izzy said Megan's missing, and that you wanted me to call. I'm not sure what I can tell you. I haven't seen her in a couple of days."

"That's fine. Did you talk to her today?"

"No. We went to dinner two nights ago, and she told me

she was going home, then spent yesterday packing. We texted back and forth some and made tentative plans for me to visit. She texted me when she got there around lunch today."

"Danny, this is Sheriff Lattimer. Have you had any contact with Burke Anderson?"

The young man uttered a soft oath. "You think he took her? That doesn't surprise me. He's a nutball and a half."

"Have you had any recent contact with him?" she asked.

"I saw him outside my apartment after my date with Megan. I think he followed me home. Other than the scene he made on our date earlier this week, he hasn't talked to me."

"Okay. If you hear from either of them, call Jasper back, or you can call my office in Pine Ridge."

"Okay. Should I come up there?"

"You can if you want," Jasper said. "You and Izzy, both. Megan might appreciate the support no matter what we find at the accident site. I'm hoping she just wandered away from her car for some reason."

"Me too. I'll call Izzy back. We'll see you soon."

"Sounds good. Bye." Jasper hung up and growled. "This just doesn't make any sense. He's never been violent. Just annoying. And he only got possessive when she started dating Danny."

"Filing that restraining order so soon after she started seeing someone else could have set him off. Either of them alone could be enough. And let's not jump to conclusions. Maybe it was him that she collided with. But maybe he just wanted to talk. It could be she ran away in fear and he followed her. We don't know that he hit her with the intention of kidnapping her."

Jasper chewed on the corner of his mouth, his dark brows drawn together. "Yeah."

She slowed as they neared the accident site, turning off her siren. Flashing lights from her car and the other responding vehicles bounced off the trees. "You don't sound convinced."

"I just can't see her running away. She'd kick his ass before she'd run. Megan knew how to defend herself. I made sure of that when she started talking about college in high school. And she embraced the training. She wouldn't run."

Katy pulled off the road behind another cruiser. She shut off the engine. "Let's go see what the scene tells us."

Thirty-Eight

The flash of red and blue emergency lights shined off the twisted metal of the cars blocking the road. Jasper heard the voice of the other cops and ambulance personnel on the scene, but nothing they said registered. His entire being was locked on his sister's car. Katy's face appeared in his line of vision, blocking the sight. He blinked and looked at her. The wind blew her blonde hair in thin wisps around her face.

"Are you okay?" Her light brown eyes narrowed in concern.

"No. But I'm okay enough to do what needs to be done. Let's go talk to your deputies and see what they've found so far."

She studied him for another moment, then gave a succinct nod. "Okay." Spinning on her heel, she led him toward the throng of people surrounding the cars.

"Goodman."

The deputy turned at the sound of his name. His eyes flicked to Jasper with a frown.

"You remember Jasper Hendriks?"

Goodman nodded.

"The Highlander driver is his sister."

The confusion on the man's face cleared, and he nodded. "Got it."

"Fill us in. Any leads on either driver?"

"Not really. Your sister's purse is still in her car, along with her phone. We didn't find anything in the other vehicle to indicate who was driving."

"We think it's her ex-boyfriend, Burke Anderson. He's been harassing her." Katy glanced around. "Have you started a search?"

"We canvassed the immediate area, but didn't go too far. I didn't want to mess up a scent trail if you brought in a K-9."

"You mind if I take a look?" Jasper itched to start searching. Whatever reason they left the scene, he wanted to find them. Now.

Katy glanced up at him. "Go ahead. I know you'll see things we won't."

He gave a curt nod, then looked at Goodman. "You have a flashlight I can borrow?" He'd soon need it in the growing darkness.

"Yeah." The man walked to his cruiser parked on the side of the road and took a long flashlight from the back and passed it to him.

"I'll walk with you." Katy took her small flashlight from her belt and glanced up at him.

Jasper nodded. Her expression told him she was going whether he liked it or not. But he didn't mind. Her police and medical expertise could come in handy. "Let's go."

He walked up to Megan's car, examining the area around her door. Glass littered the roadway. It looked like it broke inward when she was hit. That Burke bumped her from behind, then she spun around, and he T-boned her.

"Look at this." He crouched down and pointed to the glass. There were places where it left long scuffs on the pavement. "Something ground it into the road, then slid." He looked away from the car, noting several similar scuffs. "They went that way." He pointed toward the Honda. His gut churned as he realized Burke likely dragged Megan from the car, intending to drive away with her. At least he knew she wasn't hurt badly enough in the accident to not be able to fight back.

"He probably put her in his car, then realized it was too damaged to drive." Katy looked around. "So, where did they go from here?"

Jasper was already walking the perimeter of the Pilot as she talked. There wasn't any glass to track this time, so he moved around it in widening circles until he reached the edge of the road. A footprint, deeper than the rest and with a different tread, marred the sandy dirt where the pavement met grass. "There."

Katy stopped beside him and shone her smaller flashlight on it. "How do you know it's not from one of my deputies?"

"It's a different tread. Your deputies are all wearing boots. This is from a sneaker. It's also deeper than I'd expect from a man of Burke's size. I think he was carrying her." He shone his light into the copse of trees. A lot of the land up here was prairie, but because of the river through this area, it was more wooded. "We need to go in there." He ground his back molars. "Dammit, I need my gear."

"Call Asa. Have him bring it to you. We're only about five miles from the ranch."

He hesitated only a moment. The desire to charge into the trees and find his sister was overruled by his need to be prepared. It wouldn't do him any good if he found her, then couldn't get them to safety because he didn't have the right stuff.

Removing his phone from his pocket, he called Asa and told him what happened, then asked him to bring his SAR supplies and some rope. Hanging up, he looked at Katy. "He said to give him ten minutes. Let's walk in there a ways and see how obvious their trail is." He figured he'd walk for five minutes, then turn around. It would give him a good idea of how easy it would be to track them.

Katy nodded and yelled at Goodman to keep an eye out for Asa, then motioned Jasper toward the trees.

He kept his light trained on the ground and walked to the side of the trail he could see in the underbrush. It was still fresh, so the ground cover hadn't rebounded from the weight passing over it. "We're not very far behind them. Keep track of the time, would you? I only want to walk for about five minutes so we can meet Asa when he arrives."

Watch beeps sounded behind him as Katy set a timer. He kept his eyes on the trail. They reached the river just as it went off. A flurry of footprints on the bank—two sets—told him Megan was under her own power. It bothered him that she hadn't gotten away. He either had a weapon, or she was too injured to fight. Shining his light along the bank, he saw the prints continue into the darkness. "They haven't crossed. At least not here." He turned to Katy. "Let's get back to the road."

They hurried up the hill, emerging just as Asa's truck came to a halt on the bridge. He hopped out and climbed into the bed, lifting a plastic tote and two bundles of rope over the side. "I think this is everything you asked for. Any word?"

Jasper took the items and tore the lid off the tub, taking out the backpack. "No, but I did a quick survey of their trail off-road. It should be easy to follow. He's not being very careful." He opened the pack to see a variety of protein heavy foods and some water bottles inside, along with his normal survival gear.

"So, he definitely kidnapped her?"

"I think so, yes. Megan would have stayed with her car. If

she chased after him or he chased her, I'd see two trails, but there's only one. They're together." His eyes found Katy's. Her grim nod was her only acknowledgment of his words. He prayed Burke didn't have a weapon. That Megan was injured, and that's why she wasn't fighting him. There wasn't any blood in her car, but that didn't mean she couldn't have broken bones slowing her down.

He buckled the helmet and ropes to his backpack, then stuffed his climbing harness inside it. Sliding it over his shoulders, he shrugged to adjust its weight, then buckled the waist strap. He hoped he wouldn't need the climbing gear down here, but there were no guarantees. The land around here liked to just drop off into ravines.

"I'm coming with you. Let me get a medical bag from the paramedics and we can go."

"What?" His hand on her arm stopped her. "What about scene coordination? Someone needs to be up here in case I need help."

"Hughes can do it. I'm not leaving you alone out there, Jazz, so forget it. I have a gun and medical training. If he's armed, I'd rather it just be the two of us and not you, a deputy, and an unarmed medic. I'd rather you not go at all, but I know that's not happening."

No, there wasn't any way short of knocking him out and tying him up that she could get him to stay behind. And while he understood her logic for wanting to accompany him, he didn't like it any more than she liked him going. But he wouldn't stop her, because he trusted her. "Fine. Get your gear."

She ran off, leaving him with Asa. The other man took in the activity around them, then looked at Jasper.

"Katy's good at her job, Jazz. And so are you. You'll get her back."

"I know." Any other option wasn't acceptable. "I just don't like putting Katy in danger."

Asa snorted, smiling. "Then you picked the wrong woman, my friend."

"Don't I know it. But we can't help who we love." It still bothered him that she put herself in danger on a daily basis, but he was dealing with it. She'd even shown up at his house a few days ago with a scuff on her cheek from a fight with a drunk suspect, and he'd just grabbed her a bag of peas, then chased the ache away with a night of intense lovemaking.

He fought back a grin. While he still didn't like that she was hurt, he definitely didn't mind the aftermath.

"I'm ready." Katy jogged up, wearing a red backpack with a white medical symbol emblazoned on it.

"Good."

Asa held out a hand. "Good luck. Let me know if there's anything I can do. Anything you need, name it and I'll get it here."

Jasper shook his hand. "I appreciate it." He looked at Katy and motioned toward the trees. "Let's go."

They took off down the route they canvassed before, following the path to the river. There, Jasper followed the river bank for another hundred yards before it looped back up the hill.

"Where the hell is he going?" Katy looked around. "It's not back to the road. Is he trying to get them lost?"

Jasper let out a snort. "I think he just doesn't know anything about being out in the wilderness." He shined his light on the obvious trail and started walking again.

Darkness fell around them, casting long shadows as the sun set. Above them, some light lingered, but beneath the emerging tree canopy, blackness enveloped them. They both kept their lights pointed low, trying to limit the light pollution. If Burke had a weapon, they didn't want to alert him to their presence.

"Are we walking in circles?" Katy asked. "I feel like we're walking in circles."

Jasper paused. "No." He held up the compass in his hand. "We're heading steadily back to town. Everything just looks the same in the dark."

A muffled shriek split the air, sharp against the backdrop of insects and night birds. Jasper spun toward the sound, his heart in his throat.

"This way." Katy took off through the trees. She had her gun in her hand, pointed at the ground as she ran.

A man shouted, then they heard a feminine grunt. Jasper's blood boiled. If Burke hurt her, he'd bury the younger man. He didn't care if Katy arrested him. No one hurt his baby sister.

Megan shrieked again, closer. Jasper shined his light into the trees, not caring if they were seen. He and Katy were making so much noise crashing through the underbrush they no longer had any element of surprise. "Megan?" His voice echoed through the forest.

"Jasper!"

Her frightened shout helped him pinpoint their location. He turned his light just to the left. Thirty yards away, he could make out the shapes of two people struggling. "There!"

Katy veered off. "Police! Freeze!" She raised her gun as she advanced. Jasper, unarmed, stayed behind her, out of the line of fire.

Burke turned, holding Megan's arm. He pointed a gun at her chest. "Back off! Back off, she's mine!" His eyes were wild in the lights.

Jasper froze as he got a good look at the maniacal expression on the kid's face. He'd lost touch with reality.

"Hey." Katy patted the air with one hand. "Let's all calm

down, okay? Burke, why don't you let Megan go and we can talk?"

"No! She's mine. You just want to keep us apart. Everyone wants to keep us apart! I won't let you. No one else deserves her. No one will treat her better than me."

Jasper bit his tongue to keep back a smart retort. It wouldn't help. Instead, he let Katy handle things.

"Are either of you hurt? Your cars both have some decent damage."

"I am." Megan's words cut off sharply with a soft wail of pain as Burke shook her.

"Shut up. We're fine." He glanced back at Katy. "I'll take care of her once I get us back to town."

"Burke, where are you going to go when you get there? You crashed your car. You're an hour away from your apartment. There are no taxi services in Pine Ridge."

His eyes darted around and a small frown formed between them as he tried to process her logic. But he shook his head. "No. Someone will give us a ride." He nodded, more to affirm to himself that he was right than to them.

"I can't let you threaten anyone else with a gun. You need to put it down and come with us. I'm sure Megan would be much more willing to hear you out if you didn't have a gun pressed to her side. Right, Megan?"

The young woman blinked twice, processing the subtle suggestion in Katy's voice. Jasper saw her eyes clear, and she nodded.

"She's right, Burke. Please, let's go with them. I promise we can talk. Really talk. Please. My ankle really hurts."

Jasper clenched his fists. Every instinct he had wanted him to charge over there and deck the kid. Only the handgun he held to Megan's side stopped him.

"Burke, if Megan keeps walking, she could do permanent

damage to her ankle. You don't want that. You love her, right? Let us help her."

"You'll take her away from me."

"Only to fix her ankle. She'll come talk to you once she's been treated."

"I will, Burke. Please."

He shifted from foot to foot. His eyes mimicked his movements, flicking from Jasper to Katy and back. Jasper tried to keep his expression clear, but wasn't entirely sure he succeeded. The desire to knock the kid's teeth out was strong.

Burke wavered. Megan must have felt his grip loosen, because she jerked her arm free and elbowed him in the gut.

"No!" Jasper lunged forward but could only watch in slow-motion as Burke stumbled back. His gun arm raised as he fell, but he had enough wherewithal to aim. In the bright light from Katy's flashlight, he saw betrayal twist the young man's expression as he stared at Megan just before he fired.

Katy's blonde hair fanned out in a curtain as she dove in front of Megan. The impact of the bullet turned her body mid-air, and she landed half on her back.

Jasper continued past her, landing on Burke as the kid sat up and shot again. A hot, searing pain set his arm on fire, but he ignored it. Grabbing Burke's wrist in his left hand, he easily held it pointed away, then hit him square in the jaw with a right cross. The younger man's head whipped to the side, and he grunted as his eyes rolled up. Jasper hit him again in the eye, and he dropped the gun.

"Roll him over." Katy stumbled up, her handcuffs dangling from her hand.

He rolled the kid away from his gun and pulled his hands behind his back. Katy snapped the cuffs over his wrists, then sank onto her butt in the dirt, clutching her side.

Jasper moved off of Burke, picking up his dropped flashlight. His eyes widened when the beam landed on Katy. He hurried to her side. "Jesus, Katy." Blood soaked the right side of her shirt below her vest. "How bad is it?"

"Not sure. I know he missed the vest. Hurts like a bitch." Flinching, she pulled on the vest's velcro straps and let it slide off.

He batted her hands away as she went to lift her t-shirt and lifted the fabric away to see a hole about an inch from the edge of her side seeping blood. His heartbeat quickened, and he turned her to look at her back. Another hole oozed blood. "It went through." His eyes widened. "It went through."

They both turned to look at Megan. She sat on the ground, but appeared unhurt.

"Megs, are you okay?" Jasper rose to run to her side. He helped her stand.

"I think so. It's just my ankle."

Katy snorted. "And here I thought I was saving you."

He glanced back to see her wince and cover her side.

Megan pulled away from him and limped to Katy's side, falling down beside her. "Thank you." She yanked Katy into a fierce hug.

"Oh!" Katy winced, but hugged her back. "You're welcome. I'm glad you're okay." She pulled back, pressing a hand to her side again. "We need to take care of our injuries, then get the heck out of here." She looked up at Jasper and extended a hand. "Help me up."

He reached for her hand. She took it, eyes widening as he pulled her to her feet and her light bounced off his body. "You're bleeding too!" Her fingers went to the hole in his shirt. "He shot you." Brows dipping, she turned to glare at the young man lying on his belly in the dirt. "You shot him?" Katy harrumphed and turned away again, removing her backpack, then kneeling to rummage through it.

Jasper crouched next to her. "Take care of yourself first. Your wound is the worst."

She frowned at him.

He just stared back. "Don't argue with me."

"Fine." She huffed. "But you're going to have to help me. I can't reach the back."

He let his knees drop to the ground and took the gauze pads she held out. He helped her clean and pack the wounds, then wrapped a heavy bandage around her side. Once she was bandaged, he let her work on his arm. It got much the same treatment hers did.

"You're not going to be able to do much lifting until that heals," she said, putting the wrappers and used gauze into a plastic bag.

He frowned, eyeing the bandage, then shrugged. "I figure I'm due a vacation after all this. We both are."

A grin slashed her face. "Agreed." She took an ace bandage from her bag and got up, walking over to where Megan sat next to a fallen log. "Let me see that ankle."

Megan pointed to her right foot. "It's that one. It got caught between the pedals when I spun around and he hit my side."

"Jazz, hold the light down here." Katy pointed to his sister's foot.

Jasper pointed his flashlight where she indicated. Katy eased Megan's canvas tennis shoe and sock off, then pulled up the bottom of her legging. Deep purple bruising discolored the inner side of her ankle and instep. The entire joint was swollen.

"How did you stay upright, let alone walk as far as you did?" Katy started wrapping her foot.

"He held me up for most of the way. I did my best to slow him down. Just before you found me, he got tired of it and made me pick up the pace. It just hurt too much. Do you think it's broken?"

A frown marred Katy's face. "Maybe. It definitely needs xrayed."

Megan grimaced, but nodded.

Katy secured the bandage, then glanced at Jasper. "We need to make sure Burke doesn't have any injuries, then make a plan to get out of here. Do you think you can get us back to the accident site in the dark?"

"I got us down here. I'll just follow the trail backwards." He helped her to her feet, and they went over to check on Burke. He'd rolled to his side, but hadn't sat up.

Katy shined her light on his face. "You have any injuries I need to patch up before we move?"

"Just my face from where Paul Bunyan there hit me."

"Buddy, you're lucky there was nothing in my hands when I swung, or you wouldn't be talking." Jasper's low growl made the young man shut up.

Crouching, Katy probed his face. "It's just bruised." She stood and turned to Jasper again. "Let's get moving."

"Do you have a signal on your radio?"

She nodded. "I should."

"Call the accident scene. I want to send up a flare and see if they can tell us how far we are from them and from the road down here. It might be quicker to hike to the road than back up the way we came."

"I need to report that we found them, anyway." She unclipped her radio from her belt and called her deputies.

Goodman's voice came over the line. "Sheriff? We heard gunshots. Everyone okay? Over."

"Sort of. Nothing lethal. We found Megan and Burke. He's been apprehended. Jasper's going to send up a flare. Can you send a deputy toward town? I think the plan is to hike directly toward the road and shorten our distance to help."

Jasper nodded.

"We need to know how far we are from it, though. Over."

"I'll go. Give me a few minutes. Over."

"Copy."

While they waited, Jasper dug water from his backpack and passed bottles around. He even helped Burke take a drink. Once they were hydrated and several minutes had passed, he took the flare gun from his bag and loaded a shell into it.

Moving away from the others, he glanced up at the tree-tops, looking for the best place to fire the flare. He didn't want to set the forest on fire by hitting the branches and having it fall back down.

Finding a clearing, he raised the gun. "Flare!" He pulled the trigger. Bright reddish-orange light shot into the night sky, illuminating the area. As it cleared the treetops, darkness descended on them again, but not as absolute as before. An eerie glow persisted as the flare shone bright above them, the light filtering down.

Katy's radio crackled to life.

"Sheriff, I see your flare. You're about half a mile from the road. Over."

"Copy. We'll head that way. Thanks, Goodman. Lattimer out."

Jasper took the compass from his pocket. He'd kept a general compass bearing in his head as they searched, but he wanted to make sure he hadn't gotten turned around in the dark. They needed to go north to reach the road. The needle spun until it pointed north. "That way." He pointed to his left.

Katy got to her feet, then helped Megan up as she looked at him. "I'll help her if you take Burke. I won't be able to hold him if he tries something."

It was probably a good thing it was dark. The menacing smile that spread over his face might have frightened them all. He grabbed Burke's arm and hauled him to his feet. "Go ahead and try something." His voice was a low growl. "I'd love nothing more than to stop you." He turned on his flashlight, adding some light to his face so the kid could see his expression.

Burke's Adam's apple bobbed, and he gave a shaky nod.

Jasper pulled him forward, shining the light at Katy and his sister. "You two ready?"

They nodded.

"Then let's go." He motioned them ahead of him. He didn't want to outpace them. Plus, he wanted to keep an eye on Katy. They'd packed her wound well, but with all the movement and the strain of having to help Megan walk, he doubted the bleeding would stop. The last thing they needed was her passing out. He couldn't carry her and control Burke. Thankfully, they only had half a mile to go.

The terrain through the woods was fairly flat, but it was littered with branches and fallen trees. It took them twice as long to hike the distance as it should have, but they made it. Once on the roadway, Katy helped Megan sit, then radioed for pickup.

Jasper breathed a sigh of relief when he saw the flashing lights of a cruiser heading toward them minutes later. In moments, Goodman pulled up, closely followed by Chief Deputy Hughes and an ambulance. It was over. They were all safe.

THIRTY-NINE

Weariness weighed on Katy's limbs as she sank into the mound of pillows on her bed. It dipped as Jasper got in next to her.

"Megan get settled okay?" They'd all come back to Katy's after being released from the hospital. It was closer than Jasper's place, and they were all dead tired.

"Yeah. She's got everything she could need for the rest of the night. The only way she'll have to get up is if she needs to use the restroom, and I left her crutches within easy reach so she could."

Katy nodded, yawning. "Good." The young woman had been lucky. She came away from the whole ordeal with just a bad ankle sprain and some minor cuts and bruises. It could have been far worse.

Jasper snapped off the bedside light and burrowed deeper into the blankets, pulling her to his side. Katy tucked her head into the crook of his shoulder and breathed in his scent, letting it envelop her. He kissed the top of her head.

"I love you, Katydid. Get some sleep."

She'd heard those three lovely words many times since he first said them. The reply rattled around in her brain each time, but she could never make the words come out. Guilt always made her smile, then look away. She knew it bothered him that she hadn't said the words back. She wanted to, but something always held her tongue. Saying the words made it real. It meant vulnerability.

But she was already vulnerable. He held her heart whether she said the words or not. And she was going to lose him if she didn't say them back.

Sitting up, she crawled over him.

"Katy? What are you doing?"

She turned on the light, then sat back down on her side of the bed to look at him. "I need to say something."

"Okay?" A cute, confused frown marred his forehead. "Can't it wait until morning? We're both exhausted."

"No. No, I need to say it now. I should have said it weeks ago."

He stilled. "Said what?"

"I love you, Jasper. I have since the day we made love the first time. I realized it on the way to the ranch. But I couldn't say the words. I tried. Vulnerability—it's not something I wear well. I don't like the way it makes me feel. But I've realized something. I've been equating emotional vulnerability with physical vulnerability. That day my squad was ambushed—I've never felt so vulnerable. And people I cared about died. Since then, I don't think I've allowed myself to love anyone else I didn't already. Not until you."

Tears welled in her eyes, and she sniffed. "I don't want to live in fear. Tonight taught me something." She wiped at her face.

He reached out and traced the wet trail. "What did it teach you, Katydid?"

She wrapped her hand around his. "That love doesn't make you vulnerable. It makes you stronger. Neither of us gave a thought to ourselves when we took down Burke. It was all about saving the ones we love. And I love you. And your sister. I want both of you in my life. Always."

The smile he gave her lit up the room more than the lamp. "I'm not going anywhere. I told you before, you're stuck with me. I meant it."

She cupped the side of his face and leaned in. "I'm glad. I want to be stuck with you. You're a good man, Jasper Hendriks. Any woman would be lucky to call you hers. I'm glad it's me." She kissed him.

His hand threaded into her hair as he kissed her back. Her body heated, but he soon gentled the kiss and pulled back. "How soon until you're well enough we can celebrate your epiphany?"

Katy chuckled. "A couple weeks. But don't worry." She leaned in again and pecked his lips. "I'll make it worth the wait."

"Yeah?" His eyes turned that steely blue she loved.

"Oh yeah."

～

The End

Thank you for reading *Katydid*, book 4 in the *Pine Ridge* series. I hope you enjoyed it and will leave a rating or review. There is a bonus scene available for this book that is exclusive to newsletter subscribers. Visit: https://ashleyaquinn.com/bonuscontent to sign up, if you haven't already joined. If you have, follow the link to download your bonus content!

For a sneak peek at book 5 in the series, *Homespun*, keep reading.

Prefer to dive right in? Follow the link below!
https://geni.us/CWnmL3R

Chapter 1

The warm late-May sunshine beat down on Alice Duvall's neck as she carried a box of pottery supplies to the trailer attached to her brother Knox's truck. She climbed inside and set it on the growing stack, then stepped out, lifting her face to the sun. The weather was nice today for her move, which made her happy. Rain and clay did not mix. Neither did rain and cardboard. Sighing, she went back inside to get another box.

"Ready?" Knox and their friends Brady and Thomas Archer stood around her kiln, preparing to move it.

Brady nodded and put a shoulder into the oven, tipping it enough for Knox and Thomas to slide a wide strap under it. They'd brought in an engine hoist to get it out of the building and onto the truck.

"Okay, you can let it down." Thomas stepped back and nodded to his brother.

"Christ, Alice. Did you buy the heaviest one on the market?" Brady huffed as he let the kiln settle on the floor. He walked around to the other side, prepared to tip it again.

She crossed her arms and leaned a shoulder against the

wall. "Not even close." A smile crossed her pretty face. "And why are you complaining? You know you're having fun showing off your he-man side." The man was a brute. At six-foot-seven, he had several inches on either of the other men, as well as fifty pounds of muscle.

Knox and Thomas chuckled as Brady rolled his eyes. "Let's get this thing on the truck so we can focus on the other stuff." He put his shoulder into the kiln. "For a single woman, you have a lot of crap."

Alice shrugged. "Art isn't cheap."

Brady grunted. "You two ready?" He looked at his brother and Knox.

They nodded, and he pushed. Once the second strap was in place, Brady set the kiln down, then Knox gathered the straps on top of it and attached them to the hoist.

"Moment of truth. I hope this works." He grasped the lever on the back of the stand and pushed. The kiln lifted. Brady and Thomas slid a third, wider strap underneath, going the opposite direction of the other two. Knox set it down again, so they could hook the strap to the hoist. Once they were all secure, he pushed on the lever once more, raising it high enough to clear the threshold.

At the door, they turned it, setting it just inside the door. They would have to unhook it to get the stand over the threshold and outside. It was quite a process, but they finally got the kiln into the trailer.

Thomas stepped out and wiped his forehead on his shoulder. "I'm glad I don't have to do that again." He slapped Knox on the shoulder. "I hope you have some strong friends in Pine Ridge."

Knox pressed his lips together, amusement lighting his eyes. "I think we've got it covered."

Alice chuckled. They did indeed. Their friend Asa Mitchell was nearly as big as Brady. Plus, he had some large ranch hands who would be more than willing to show off their strength. "I'm just glad I have friends on both ends willing to help." She smiled at Brady and Thomas.

"Hey, you offered to pay me in food." Thomas walked past her, glancing back. "I won't turn that down." His mouth twisted. "Especially since Rayna hates meat right now. I can't wait until she's past the stage where the smell of cooking meat makes her want to puke. It's been beans and tofu and lots of vegetables for the last two months." He waved a hand. "I'm not really complaining, though. I'll eat whatever keeps her stomach happy."

Alice wrinkled her nose. That sounded terrible. "Is she doing okay otherwise?"

He nodded. "She's doing great. The baby's growing well. Mason and Emma are excited to have a little brother or sister. Especially Emma. She can't wait to babysit."

Her heart warmed at the mention of his adopted children. Those kids, especially Mason, deserved every happiness in the world after what they'd been through. "Good. I'll have to come visit once he or she arrives." She hadn't seen much of Rayna lately. The other woman had been busy prepping her fields for the growing season and packing up their old house to move onto the ranch.

"We both will," Knox said. "Sofie and I can introduce our little one to yours. They'll be about the same age." Knox's wife was only a couple of months further along in her pregnancy than Rayna.

Alice smiled at her brother, happy for him. He'd been alone for a long time before Sofie came into his life. The change in him was drastic. He smiled more and didn't hide away like he used to. She was looking forward to living close to him again. She couldn't wait to spoil his new baby and his five-year-old stepdaughter, Olive.

They spent the next hour loading boxes from her pottery

studio into the trailer. Once they were done, they left the trailer and the truck attached to it where it was, and piled into Alice's Subaru. She'd promised them all supper from Boone's for their trouble.

As she drove off the ranch, she couldn't help the melancholy that flooded her heart. This place had been her home since she was a kid until she bought her own house in town when she started teaching art at the elementary. After their mom died and their dad moved away, it was just Knox's home until a fire destroyed his horse barn and he decided to move his family to Pine Ridge to be closer to Sofie's mom. Alice had been a frequent visitor to the old ranch, though, thanks to the pottery studio they'd built on the grounds.

But now, the ranch belonged to Thomas and Rayna, and it was time for a new era for Alice. Sure, she'd miss her friends here, but Montana wasn't that far from Colorado. And she wanted to be near her brother and his growing family. She wanted to watch her niece and this new baby grow up. And maybe she'd meet someone to share her life with. Heaven knew her prospects around here weren't great. All the good men were taken, or she wasn't interested.

Not that she was in any rush. She was twenty-nine. But she was definitely ready for a family of her own.

"Alice, you need a bigger car," Thomas complained from the backseat.

She looked in the rearview mirror to see him glance at Knox.

"How come you get to sit behind her, and I'm stuck behind The Hulk?" He pointed at Brady, who sat in the front passenger seat.

Knox snorted. "Because I'm taller than you." She felt him shift behind her, his knees bumping her seat.

"By an inch."

He shrugged.

Alice chuckled. "I can turn around, and you can take your own truck to town."

Thomas waved a hand, a light smile on his handsome face. "Nah. I just like giving Brady a hard time." He pushed on the seat.

Brady barely moved, but a grin tilted one side of his mouth. "Watch it, or I'll sit on you."

"You wouldn't fit back here."

"Who says it has to be now?"

Alice glanced in the mirror again and caught Knox's eye. They shared a smile as they listened to the brothers' banter. These two and the rest of their family would be the people she missed the most. Especially their sister, Maggie. She was just glad she'd gotten all her goodbyes out of her system over the weekend. She didn't want to drive away tomorrow morning with tears in her eyes.

They reached town, and Alice steered the car through the quaint residential streets to the downtown area and parked. Thomas and Knox both let out groans as they unfolded themselves from the backseat. Alice led the way into the restaurant. A hostess led them to a booth by the window. They soon ordered, then sat back to wait for their food. Several people stopped to say hello to Knox and inquire about his family and how they were settling in up north.

When their food arrived, the three men inhaled their dinner. Alice refused to eat so fast she barely tasted her burger, especially since it was the last one she'd have from Boone's for a while. The others didn't seem to mind waiting on her, though. They sat there and talked while she finished.

Once they were done, they piled into the car again and drove back to the ranch so Thomas and Brady could get their trucks and head home. She tried to keep the tears at bay as she said goodbye to the men. She was going to miss them—all the Archers, really.

Sniffing, she hugged them, then waved as they drove away. Knox wrapped an arm around her shoulders, and she leaned into him.

"You know, as much as I'm sad you're leaving your friends behind, I'm glad you're moving up north with me and Sofie. It'll be great still having you close by."

Alice nodded. "Yeah. And it's not like we're saying goodbye to them forever." Between Knox's business dealings with them and their own personal history, she knew they'd be frequent visitors to each other's homes over the years to come.

Knox nodded. "Definitely not." He gave her a squeeze. "Come on. Let's head inside. Thomas left us a television. Want to watch something with me before we hit the sack? I bet we can find reruns of some sitcom to watch."

She smiled up at him and wiped her face. "Sure." Maybe a few episodes of *The Big Bang Theory* or even *Golden Girls* would cheer her up. Following him inside, she pressed a fist to her chest, holding back the melancholy.

They stopped in the kitchen and got themselves each a bottle of water, then sat down on the couch in the living room. Thomas and Rayna had moved a few things in, so Knox and Alice had a place to stay while they moved Alice out of her house. There were two beds upstairs as well.

Knox grabbed the remote off the coffee table and turned on the TV. He flipped through the channels until he found one playing a marathon of *The Big Bang Theory*. Alice sank deeper into the cushions, pulling her legs beneath her. As the show played, she felt herself relax, some of the sadness creeping away, thanks to the humor of the show. After the fourth episode, she stretched and yawned. Glancing at her brother, she saw him cover his own yawn.

"We should get to bed." She uncoiled herself.

He nodded. "Yeah." Turning off the TV, he stood.

Alice rose and picked up her empty water bottle. They

tossed them in the recycling bin in the mudroom, then headed upstairs. She paused outside the room she was using. "I'll see you in the morning."

Knox glanced back, his hand on the doorknob to the master bedroom. "Bright and early." His mouth quirked.

She smiled back and went into her room. Gathering her nightclothes, she went down the hall to take a shower. Once she was clean and had brushed her teeth, she went back to her room and shut off the light, climbing between the sheets.

Fatigue pulled at her—it had been a busy day—but her mind refused to shut off. Huffing, she sat up and turned on the bedside lamp. She'd just read until she couldn't keep her eyes open anymore.

She got up and found her e-reader in her bag, then crawled back into bed. Turning it on, she immersed herself in her book.

When her head bobbed a couple of hours later, she put it down and turned off the light. Nerves still churned her belly, but exhaustion finally won, and she dropped off to sleep.

The blare of her alarm on her phone jolted her awake a few hours later. Groaning, she shut it off and sat up. She rubbed her gritty eyes and pushed her hair out of her face. With a yawn, she stretched and got out of bed and padded over to her suitcase to get some clothes. A quick trip to the bathroom to dress and do her morning routine, and she was ready to go.

Packing her suitcase, she double-checked she had everything, then zipped her bag and headed downstairs.

Knox stood at the counter, munching on a banana. He raised a brow at her and nodded in greeting.

"Mornin'." She walked straight to the coffeepot and poured some into her travel mug. She peeled the other banana, quickly eating it.

"You want one of these?" Knox held out a protein bar.

She took it. "Sure. I'll eat it in the car."

"We don't have to rush out, you know."

Alice shrugged. "No point in lingering."

He nodded. "Okay. I'm ready if you are. Let's load up."

She grabbed her bags and followed him out of the house. A wide yawn cracked her jaw as she stared out over the ranch in the early light. Gold lit the tops of the hills and the dew sparkled in the rising sun.

"None of that. We've got a long drive ahead of us and need to be alert."

Alice rolled her eyes at her brother. "That's why I have this." She held up her coffee cup, then narrowed her eyes. "Do *you* have coffee?"

He grinned. "It's already in the truck."

She smiled back. "Then let's go."

His chuckle faded as they went to their separate vehicles. Knox had driven down from Pine Ridge in his truck so he could haul the trailer back. Alice planned to follow him in her SUV.

Climbing into her car, she set her coffee in the cup holder and her purse on the passenger seat, then started the engine. Excitement zinged through her veins, battling with her nerves. This was a big move for her. She'd been praying for a way to move closer to Knox after he and Sofie announced they were moving to Pine Ridge. When the art teacher position came open at the school there, she'd jumped on it. She still couldn't believe the school board picked her.

But she was definitely more excited than nervous. This was the right move. And not just because she'd be closer to Knox. She couldn't wait to start teaching in the fall. As part of the interview process, she'd toured the school. It was a new building, and the art program had all the latest stuff. She'd have a kiln on-site. No more schlepping her students' art back and forth from school to the ranch to fire everything and praying nothing broke on the way.

Knox turned around in the wide drive in front of the ranch buildings and headed for the highway. Alice put her car in gear and followed. They turned onto the road and were off. She couldn't hold back the grin. Time for new beginnings.

~

I hope you enjoyed this sneak peek of *Homespun*. If you would like to read the next book, please visit the link below to get your copy. Thanks again for reading!

Get *Homespun*: https://geni.us/CWnmL3R

SIGN UP FOR MY NEWSLETTER!

Stay up-to-date on all the latest happenings in the Pine Ridge world by joining my newsletter. You'll also receive a **FREE** full-length e-book just for signing up! Visit ashleyaquinn.com to sign up today!

About the Author

After spending most of her adulthood moving around the U.S. and Europe, romantic suspense author Ashley A. Quinn has settled in South Dakota with her husband, two kids, and a menagerie of pets. Her first novel, *Smoky Mountain Murder*, came out in 2016, and she has since published more than two dozen books. When not writing, you can find her with her nose stuck in a romantic thriller or binge-watching British TV dramas and reality shows. She is an avid baseball fan and also enjoys growing all the things in her garden and bookbinding. To find out more about her and her books visit https://ashleyaquinn.com.

goodreads.com/ashleyaquinn

amazon.com/Ashley-A-Quinn/e/B07HCT4QST

facebook.com/ashleyaquinn.writer

instagram.com/ashleyaquinn.writer

tiktok.com/@ashleyaquinn.writer